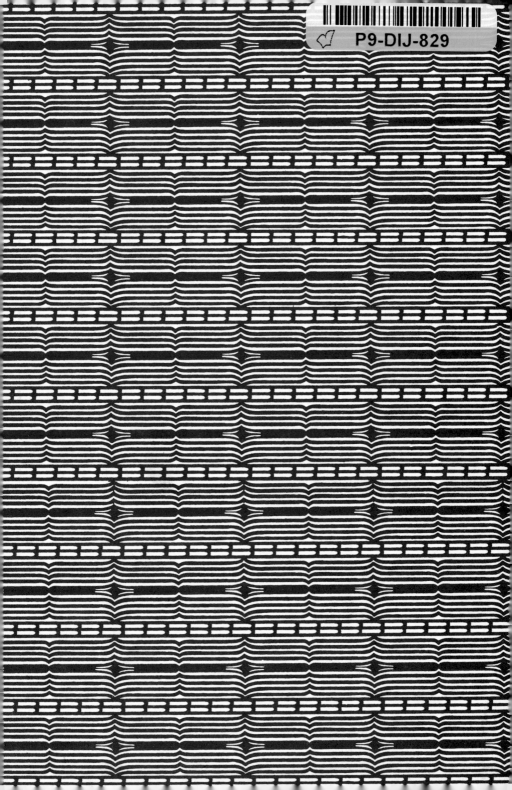

A
DESIGN
FOR
LIVING

Lillian Langseth-Christensen

A DESIGN FOR LIVING

VIKING

VIKING

Viking Penguin Inc., 40 West 23rd Street, New York, New York 10010, U.S.A.
Penguin Books Ltd, 27 Wrights Lane, London W8 5TZ
(Publishing & Editorial)
and Harmondsworth, Middlesex, England
(Distribution & Warehouse)
Penguin Books Australia Ltd, Ringwood, Victoria, Australia
Penguin Books Canada Limited, 2801 John Street,
Markham, Ontario, Canada L3R 1B4
Penguin Books (N.Z.) Ltd, 182–190 Wairau Road, Auckland 10, New Zealand

First published in 1987 by Viking Penguin Inc.
Published simultaneously in Canada

Grateful acknowledgment is made for permission to reproduce the photographs on the
following pages: 43—Klimt and his cat, from Bildarchiv der Osterreich National-
bibliothek; 132, 133, 136, 137—Hoffmann sketches, Archiv der Hochschule für angewandte
Kunst in Wien; 151—Hoffmann sterling silver dinner service, C. Hugo Pott; 158—
Portrait of Klimt, from Bildarchiv der Osterreich Nationalbibliothek; 187—Professor
Edward Wimmer, Archiv der Hochschule für angewandte Kunst in Wien; 190, 191—
Wimmer dress sketches, Archiv der Hochschule für angewandte Kunst in Wien; 201—
Emilie Flöge in a Klimt smock, from Bildarchiv der Osterreich Nationalbibliothek. All
other photographs are from the author's collection.

LIBRARY OF CONGRESS CATALOGING IN PUBLICATION DATA
Langseth-Christensen, Lillian.
A design for living.
1. Hoffmann, Josef Franz Maria, 1870–1956—Influence.
2. Wiener Werkstätte. 3. Decorative arts—Austria—
Vienna—History—20th century. 4. Vienna (Austria)—
Intellectual life. 5. Langseth-Christensen, Lillian—
Biography—Youth. 6. Authors, Austrian—20th century—
Biography—Youth. I. Title.
NK946.H63L36 1987 745.4'4924 [B] 86-40513
ISBN 0-670-80089-9

Printed in the United States of America by
Arcata Graphics, Fairfield, Pennsylvania
Set in Plantin
Designed by Francesca Belanger

FOR
CARMELA PRATI HAERDTL

Contents

A DESIGN FOR LIVING

CHAPTER 1

Discovering
Josef Hoffmann

My parents were the sort of people who went to the opera on Monday nights and I was the sort of child who could not wait for them to go. My weekly routine was always the same; as soon as they were safely out of the house, I went back to Mother's dressing room where, by a strange arrangement of six mirrors, three in front and three behind, I could see myself as others saw me. By manipulating the four side panels I had no secrets from myself, and no illusions.

It was at a time when I still had, as eight-year-old girls did in those days, long hair straight down the back and tied on top of my head with a large wilted blue bow, always blue as Mother explained because my eyes were blue. It was anchored with a barrette, which hurt, and the whole structure had a tendency to slide to one side. The rear-view mirrors made it possible to check whether my hair had grown long enough to reach my waist, not to mention that it might become long enough to sit on. Below all this I wore either a Bramley dress or a white middy blouse on which Father would not permit naval emblems, with a pleated blue serge skirt and bloomers, white socks, and very depressing flat black shoes. Rubber soles, my dearest wish, were also prohibited.

After a long scrutiny I always went on to the room that was called the library, since the walls were lined with mahogany bookcases in the Chippendale manner. The fact that our bookcases were built in, while my friends' parents' libraries contained free-standing book cabinets, was about as reassuring as an Olympic-size swimming pool, a loden green Mercedes station wagon and a Japanese gardener would be today. What little in the room was not mahogany paneling or books was a proper forest green with the exception of a beige "seamless" rug that had been woven especially by Tiffany Studios, another plus for us. There was also an enormous Edwardian library chair in tufted red hide, reserved for Father.

The library had a few sporting touches contributed by a friend of Father's who was asked to dinner once a year. On these occasions his photograph, with gun in hand, head thrown back and one foot planted on the rump of his latest moose, was slipped into a hammered silver frame in front of Grandmother's picture on the library desk. The second temporary decorating arrangement made for this annual event was the substitution of one of his stuffed golden cock pheasants, usually kept in camphor, for the enormous silver-mounted German drinking horn that stood on the dining room mantel. It was poised, illogically, on the shoulder of a prancing infant Siegfried while Gambrinus sat across a barrel on its lid.

I was ashamed that we had nothing in the way of trophies to indicate that Father was or ever had been a sportsman or a hunter, an attribute that played an important part in home decorating in 1916. He was a music-loving, wine-cellar-proud ex–Austrian cavalry officer who had come to New York to fetch Mother in 1904 and stayed ever since. He was irritable at home and charming out and he hadn't an oar, a racket or a cup to his name. There were no antlered heads in our front hall, nothing to vie with my friends' fathers' stuffed trout, team photographs or pennants. We depended for all the required furred and feathered mementos, and some incidental hampers of rather high partridge, pheasant and grouse, on Father's friend, whose wife would have none of them on walls or table.

His most important donation to our library's decor was a large moose-hide-covered hassock that stood in front of the gas-log fireplace, where a brass fender, lighter and various fireplace tools lent veracity to the three perforated asbestos pseudo-birch logs, which were cleaned with ammonia twice a year. He always smelled of cigars and gave my brother Edward and me each a twenty-dollar gold piece and these in turn were given to Father to put in our mythical savings accounts, and were never seen again.

The moose hassock was supported by three of the moose's highly polished gigantic cloven-hooved feet, cut off at the fetlock. The fourth hoof had been cleverly transformed into an inkwell with the donor's and Father's names engraved on the silver lid. The hide of the moose that had gone to make

Mother and Father ∎

these noble gifts was casually secured over the hassock with a sort of studded belt arrangement and the extra hide that hung below it was cut into an Indian-style fringe that made a modish uneven hemline from which the glossy hoof tips protruded.

The hassock stood on the skin of an adult grizzly bear, shot by the same friend. Only the head was three-dimensional and his great carnivorous jaws were wide open, with wax tongue curled back in deadly anticipation or as though he were about to say "Ah" to the doctor. But his eyes were rather sweet, dark brown glass with an unwavering glint. The rest of him was lined with brown felt and lay flat on the rug where Father always stumbled over him. The moose hassock and the bear's head were the two warmest and most comfortable places to sit for my Monday reading sessions. Light came from an inverted alabaster saucer suspended from the ceiling and imposing lamps that served no purpose since the fringes on their opaque shades were so long that they had to be combed at intervals. There were palms in jardinieres on teakwood stands, where I disposed of medications and chocolates with green marzipan centers.

I was proud of our library. It contained no stained glass, no paintings on easels draped with Spanish shawls, no fur pillows and no accessories to show where we had been, such as Leaning-Tower-of-Pisa lamps, bronze Eiffel Towers or Lions of Lucerne bookends. It was, to my mind, all in the best of taste, especially as compared with the home of one of my friends, whose parents had a library in reverse. That

6

room was all in red with a green leather Morris chair and an off-white polar bear skin on the red carpet. The bear was lined in ice-blue felt that protruded all around and had been cut in scallops with pinking shears. They had a second polar bear in alabaster, with an electric light inside him, who fished from a chunk of pink marble balanced on a white marble column. They also had an ecru-pinkish Pomeranian called Peggy.

There I sat on my fringed moose-hide hassock, on a grizzly bear skin in a cluttered library-green library in front of three hissing realistic gas logs with a petunia-shaped Victrola and a case of Caruso records in the corner and library-oriented accessories on the table behind me. There was an ivory paper knife, almost as long as the tusk from which it was cut, and a jewel-encrusted magnifying glass to match. The room was stuffed with furniture and always looked as though my parents could not only receive but seat everyone they knew at the same time. My reading, which was actually only a looking at pictures, was limited to *The Treasures of the Vatican* as all other books were in German Gothic type and concentrated on Goethe, Wagner and wine. But there were magazines on top of the bookcases that I could reach by climbing on the backs of chairs.

My parents were abandoned subscribers to everything: the Metropolitan Opera, the Philharmonic, the Philadelphia Orchestra and The Friends of Music, to every art organization and publication, many of which we could not read. The one that came from Japan started at the back and had

7

no illustrations, but it came in a silk-covered box secured with little ivory tabs. *L'Art et la Mode* and *The Studio*, with its ill-favored couple on the cover under their twisted tree, vied with *National Geographic Magazine* for first place. *Musical America* took last place. *Saint Nickolas* and *Die Woche* were sent up to the playroom to teach us the rewards that were in store for good children. We studied gnomes hiding under toadstools and the Two Grenadiers plowing their way home from Russia in a blizzard beset by wolves, and I cried over a melancholy dog that leaned against his master's headstone.

At this point I found my absolute favorite of all magazines: *Deutsche Kunst und Dekoration* (German Art and Decoration), published in Darmstadt since 1897 and full of glorious art and fascinating decoration as it was then taking place in Vienna. I was the only one who opened the German magazines and I was enthralled. The Chippendale jumble around me fell away when I saw my first plain black polished oak furniture, side chairs with high narrow backs and low seats. Whatever was not black was of glossiest white enamel, upholstered in plain leather or in fabrics woven with geometric designs. Armchairs were austere and boxlike on the outside, with softly upholstered seats and backs inside. There were glowing golden panels by Gustav Klimt, whom I remembered from Vienna in 1914, largely because of his cat, and furniture legs that did not end at the floor, but turned at right angles to meet each other. The tables were not all at a uniform dining-table height; there were low and high ta-

8

bles and I saw my first *Beistelltisch*, which is one word for a stand-by table. It was all simple and uncomplicated, new and calm, unornamented and flat with square corners, decorative and almost entirely black and white. The name under most of the photographs was J. Hoffmann.

Although I had no way of knowing anything about J. Hoffmann, not even what the "J" stood for, I was carried away with the things that he or she had designed. They went from furniture to book bindings, silver, glass and even to villas, jewelry and handbags, and from lamps, fabrics and papers to large architectural projects. There were pictures of J. Hoffmann rooms that showed an extraordinary orderliness. They reminded me of enlargements of the beautiful velvet-lined silver chests in which silversmiths housed their silver. Every fork and every knife and spoon had its fork-, knife- or spoon-shaped hollow into which it exactly fit. Nothing ever lay about; everything had its place.

Apparently J. Hoffmann, whom I began to think of as a man, did not hold with clutter. He used a few beautiful objects but isolated them in niches or on pedestals. He seemed to be an extremely orderly man, and I imagined that he met with his clients to find out just how many pairs of shoes, handkerchiefs, coffee cups, ladles and hot-water bottles they had so that he could design a place for each of them. There is an old story that I heard just recently about two friends who met in a real estate office. Since one of them had just moved into a new Hoffmann apartment, the other asked her what in the world she was doing there. The

9

answer was that she was looking for a new apartment because she could not bear to miss the pleasure of having Hoffmann doing one for her. In spite of all the order and nonclutter and the litterless look, Hoffmann rooms appeared lived-in and warm. He did not fan out his furniture all over a room; he concentrated it in suitable escape locations, as under balcony stairs, in a niche between cabinets or between stack-like enclosures, columns or dividers. Everything was built-in, enameled, flush and peaceful; pictures were apt to be grouped from floor to ceiling, or to be down near the baseboard; beds were always in alcoves, or at least their heads were in recesses. Hoffmann people could sit together in the sitting area of their sitting rooms without shouting across unoccupied chairs at each other; there was a feeling of snugness and even the chairs he designed for his clients had an embracing shape that one could get away into. One of them looked mighty like a round, mobile bird cage with an open door.

Whatever Hoffmann created was of a great and elegant simplicity; by rights it should have been unobtrusive, but instead it bombarded one with its perfectness. Everything fit into its background so perfectly that I wondered whether Hoffmann householders marked their floors with chalk, as stage floors are marked, so that everything could stand at its appointed spot. Textiles and wallpaper designs were geometric; lettering was clear and decorative; leather was plain or tooled in linear patterns. There was magnificent glass, beguiling ceramics, jewelry and devastating fashions. Everything was new, original, optimistic, clean and young. It was logical and beautiful and I could see myself slinking about in just such a setting. One photograph showed a Hoffmann client dressed in the same printed velvet that covered her chairs. J. Hoffmann, whoever he or she was, was changing the look of everything for the better.

I pored over the minutest details, the metal ferrules and the bentwood, the floor coverings and the lighting fixtures, for hours on end. My Hoffmann's rooms were large, immaculate and bare, but white walls were beautifully demarked with hairline black moldings or beadings, coffered ceilings were emphasized with narrow black and white enamel strips, and if there were paintings they were set into the paneling rather than hanging at an angle that cast triangular shadows on the wall behind them. Small groups of comfortable furniture stood isolated in what was known as a *Sitzecke*, a sitting corner (not to be confused with anything as trite as a cozy corner), or separate nests of furniture were grouped together as they might be in a hotel lounge. His interiors were islanded, not all-over designs. I visualized the European hostess, who always carried her own handbag and key ring in her own house, sitting in her appointed chair precisely where it always stood, facing the exact number of guests for whom J. Hoffmann had provided seating.

Hoffmann clients apparently cut their lives and their entertaining to fit their houses, or perhaps Hoffmann worked from specifications that read: "Provide for three ladies for tea, four groups of four for black coffee and bridge and two tête-à-tête niches." Furniture had its place and didn't get pushed around at will. I saw pictures of large rooms that contained only three or four of what was called *eine Sitzgelegenheit*, a sitting opportunity. In that case I presumed that the hostess who wanted to ask more guests than Hoffmann had placed chairs for had to give a *Lunch Debout*, a standing luncheon, or repair immediately to the dining room. Hoffmann dining rooms seemed to always be large with long narrow tables and lots of chairs. The cocktail hour did not exist and the time between arrival at the front door and seating at the table was as short as possible. From what I knew of European dining and cooks, punctuality was essential.

The name Hoffmann bothered me. Up to then I had thought that Josef Hofmann was the curly-haired pianist at whose concert my chilblains had itched and that E. T. A. Hoffmann had written the *Tales* that I was taken to hear at the Met. So the unknown Hoffmann became a mystery, a far-off ideal, the man who was going to, and did, change my world.

I rejoiced in the changes that J. Hoffmann brought about, but I did not know what he had outgrown or what his world had looked like before he changed it. For all I knew, he may have descended from upright Biedermeier forebears. There was certainly a clearer relationship between Hoffmann and the simple fruitwood furniture with ebony accents that nineteenth-century Central Europe called Biedermeier than between Hoffmann and the atrocities that were admired

12

as the century turned. That was the day when the Austrian Court, and therefore the whole Austrian upper crust, thought that the painter Hans Makart's flamboyancies were *das letzte Wort,* the last word—when dried palms, peacock feathers, bulrushes and cattails, wild animal skins, baldachins and open fans were beautiful. Perhaps Hoffmann was reacting to an aesthetic that admired rape scenes of Proserpina in bronze, crowded together with tasseled brocade and miscellaneous pieces of armor. At that time the more objects that were crowded into a room the better, and the addition of a draped Turkish corner with a tambourine turned neighbors green with envy. The *ne plus ultra* were stuffed and costumed animals bearing trays, scimitars or some of the obscurer musical instruments. In the Vienna of the later nineteenth century, a chair only became a chair when it was beaded, festooned, swagged, deeply tufted and antimacassared. A clock could be a bronze Newfoundland dog with the dial set in his side and his tail the pendulum. It was no wonder that J. Hoffmann's rooms were empty, his chairs were unrelenting, there were no divans, he provided no place to throw oneself and clock faces were dots on the wall centered with a pair of simple hands. If the owner of a Hoffmann residence had possessions, they could not be seen; everything had its place behind closed doors.

The only thing I knew of Central European decoration, where Chippendale was unknown, was gathered from our annual summer wine-buying, Grandmother-visiting trips

13

where we saw the best of European interiors in the palatial old hotels that were called, fittingly, Palace, Majestic or Imperial, all of them full of mighty marble columns, fragile bird-cage-like lifts, red velvet, gold tassels, green plush and bathtubs on clawed feet. Lamp shades looked like pink afternoon tea cakes and everything was embellished with silken ropes and cockades. My further knowledge of European home decoration came when we finally arrived in Karlsbad, at the homes of my two grandmothers, one of whom was pure Biedermeier, the other a combination of leftover Gothic (too large to move) and *Jugendstil*, as Karlsbad conceived it. Everything was done up in festoons of green velvet printed with long-stemmed red poppies, voluptuously interwoven with dandelions. Father was furious when he found the home he had grown up in alive with faux bamboo. I too was saddened; I had had my eye, ever since I could focus it, on her Biedermeier sewing box and a small fire screen.

I was too young to have any judgment; I had thought, until I discovered Hoffmann, that a stuffed red parrot in a hoop was a fetching room accessory, that anything at all under a glass dome was admirable and that having the framed photograph of a relative in presentation feathers and train was about as distinguished as one could get. As far as houses went, I had leaned toward a British vicarage style with lots of chimneys and ivy, but not after I saw Hoffmann's neat villas and pavilions, his integration of exterior and interior,

With my
walking stick
and cigarette,
just before
sailing to Vienna.
I was fourteen
at the time
and wanted
to look eighteen.

of landscape and client. It seemed to me that he designed his clients' whole lives, not merely the shells into which they moved their furniture.

The appeal of simple black and white, of lack of frippery was enormous. A new world came at me out of the pages of *Deutsche Kunst und Dekoration*, and J. Hoffmann changed from a name to a man. He was no longer young, about thirty, tall, handsome and with a slight speech impediment. I was at an age when older men who limped, wore glasses, stuttered or needed my support were far to be preferred over hale and hefty youth. I invariably selected some handicap that made them appealingly dependent but still able to dance divinely. My Hoffmann was gentle, confiding and clean-shaven. I visualized long hours of art discussions, of warm encouragement and dancing. My Hoffmann loved his pupils and they were mad about him. His school combined all the charms of a Greenwich Village tearoom, Strauss waltzes and any place that was not home in New York.

I think his attraction for me, who was nearing ten when I discovered him and fourteen when I left for Vienna to study with him, was that I found his work at a time when I was undecided about what I wanted to study or to be. I knew I wanted to study design but not which branch. Hoffmann's unlimited versatility, his all-aroundness, his equally skilled many-sidedness covered all the fields of design, and that was what I wanted to learn to be, a designer of everything.

From the first issue that I saw of *Deutsche Kunst und Dekoration*, I knew exactly where I was going and what I wanted to do and to be. I was going to Vienna to be a J. Hoffmann pupil and, being a docile as well as a determined child, who never answered unless asked, I laid my plans and waited for the question that was bound to come at some time: "And what do you want to do when you grow up?"

CHAPTER 2

Joseph Urban
Paves the Way to Vienna
and Hoffmann

Unfortunately, no one seemed the least bit interested in what I wanted to be or do when I grew up. In those days girls were girls, usually awkward, until they came out and married and that, for some reason, was that. My friends talked constantly of their debuts, their engagements, their showers and their weddings. They spoke of their dreamed-up husbands and the exact number of children they were going to have, right down to their sexes. They all said, with slight variations, "I am going to marry a lawyer (or broker), live in Greenwich (or Darien) and have two boys, a station wagon and a girl." Even their children's names, after Mummy and Daddy, or after Grandfather if he was rich, were predictable. They promised one another bridesmaidships, and each of them wanted to be the first to have all this happen to her.

None of it could erase the glowing picture of Vienna that lay ahead of me. I did not share it with anyone; I did not specify the flowers in my bridal bouquet or promise to throw it at anyone in particular from the head of the stairs. I did once ask some of my friends what they thought of the study of art as a future occupation, without mentioning where or with whom this was to take place, and was shrugged off by all of them with a "You're different." Being different was the result of having had an Austrian upbringing in New York; I called my parents Mamma and Papa instead of Mummy and Daddy, I had a German governess called Fräulein Martha and I was born in New York, whereas my schoolmates had come into the world in chic-er places, such as Morristown or Greenwich. I also spoke English English, which I had learned in London in 1914, at a time when a German-speaking child was an embarrassment.

My parents had been wildly unconventional in a staid Austrian way. Father, being an officer, could not carry parcels and Mother could not go out without gloves, but she sailed to New York alone to visit a friend in 1904, when she was tired of waiting for Father's mother's approval of a wedding date. He followed her on the next steamer and they were married the day he landed in Hoboken. All this independence went to their heads, so they honeymooned back to Austria only to tell their widowed mothers that they were going to live in New York. Edward was born there in 1906 and I followed two years later. According to a promise made before my parents left Austria, we returned there each summer and Edward and I were experienced travelers by 1914, when the outbreak of war hurled us across the map. Our household returned to New York in driblets, wearing life belts while at sea, in 1915. I think the chauffeur came first and, to our joy, the governess came last, still in her straw hat. Our parents and we came home via a cold and rain-drenched Holland to London, where we waited for passages while a Miss Simpson taught Edward and me English. It was a crash course, but since our vocabularies were small and we had to *say it in English* or not at all, we learned quickly and spoke a cross between a German and a genteel London cemetery accent.

In 1915 I was entered into something progressive that was, in those days, called an Ungraded Class. It was an early-day kindergarten where our teacher, who was basically lazy, gave us long lessons in folding our arms on our desks and putting our heads down on them while she murmured relax, relax. I think she hoped we would fall asleep. We drank milk through straws and learned to sing squeakily. I was made to do a solo of *"Stille Nacht, Heilige Nacht,"* and that with a war going on. The following years I was advanced to first and then to second grade, and from third grade, when I had discovered Hoffmann, I skipped to fifth and seventh grades, and so on. None of this was due to intelligence, only to an ability to memorize, and to remember just long enough to get by in class next day, with a picture of Vienna ahead. I not only memorized quickly, usually on the way to school, but I forgot just as quickly on my way home. Thereby I gained hours, untroubled by homework, for doodling in my school books and drawing sinuous Erté-type costume sketches.

During the four years between my discovery of Hoffmann and my departure for Vienna, Fräulein Martha left and was

replaced by a part-time Madame Blé, who ran me through Central Park every afternoon while she spoke French as rapidly as she ran. I did everything that was considered part of a proper schoolgirl's education—took piano lessons, rode at Durland's Riding Academy, had drawing lessons from Thomas Furlong and was taken to Burton Holmes's travel lectures with black and white slides. I was taken to Walter Damrosch's Saturday morning Music Appreciation sessions, where I was found to be hopelessly unappreciative. Most torturous of all were ballroom dancing lessons where Edward, down from school for weekends, shone in serge and white gloves while I, in Alice-blue taffeta, barely managed the closing polonaise. Since Mother was born in the center of Europe, far from deep water, we took swimming lessons together in Annette Kellermanns (advanced one-piece bathing suits), doing the breast stroke conscientiously across a New York pool.

Wartime summers were spent in Norfolk, Connecticut, which didn't have all that Bayreuth would have offered Father, but there was a Music Festival and conductor Artur Bodanzky came to stay. Edward and I completed the outdoor side of our educations. We rode, were given golf and tennis lessons—fruitfully for Edward, uselessly for me—and I struggled around with water wings in shallow water.

■ Edward, when he was at Princeton
and I was in Vienna

21

While our parents entertained Music Festival musicians, we played with the Julian Street children and my cocker spaniel Christmas collected burrs, broke his leg and mistakenly shared Bodanzky's hairbrush all summer.

Life was happy and simple for the simple reason that I never spoke, or hardly ever, and when I did it was in a whisper. I walked on tiptoes because I was that sort of child and I never rocked the boat. Artur Bodanzky always shouted *"Don't make so much noise!"* when I hadn't peeped in hours. In autumn Edward went back to boarding school and I returned to my library reading and my accumulated German magazines. No one knew that I knew where I was going and what I was going to do. I can only remember now that I wanted to get away from New York and the finishing schools and coming-outs that loomed, but mostly I wanted to study with J. Hoffmann in Vienna. Although I had no clear picture of what I would do in the future with what he taught me, or of how his school functioned, I was still determined to get into it at all costs. Evenings, when my parents were at home, I peered over the bannister at their guests critically, and listened in on the enlightening things they said on arrival, and again on their way down to dinner after drinking Father's newfangled cocktail concoctions. I listened to their bursts of laughter and ate elaborately off trays that were brought up to me at intervals. I was a schoolgirl in a Bramley dress, a two-piece jersey dress with pleated skirt, the jeans of the twenties, who dined off the last of the caviar-filled *profiteroles*, ate soups that were mostly sherry, loved beautiful pompano sizzling under anchovy butter or shad roe smothered in pimiento julienne and cream. Elaborately garnished fillets or saddles followed and the desserts, all great successes with the operatic friends (most of whom were overweight, as I was in a splendid position to judge from above), were flamed or spun-sugared elaborations. Sometimes, by special Austrian request, it was a sugared horseshoe of an *Apfelstrudel*, with a caramelly end for me. When my parents were out, I ate rice pudding by request— not the soupy kind, but kernelly with lots of raisins and raspberry sauce. When my parents were home without guests, the three of us ate Father's diet and went irritably to bed.

After my gala trays or my library magazine reading, after lovely rice puddings, I took my bath and dressed, including hat, shoes and gloves, put a loaded water pistol under my pillow with which to shoot burglars and climbed into bed with my books. This made it possible for me to read half the night, sleep more than an hour longer in the mornings, dump the contents of my breakfast tray down the john and still get to school on time.

Deutsche Kunst und Dekoration had shown me how a bedroom should look. It was no longer a place for a bed, a night table, a chiffonier that was too high to look into the top drawer, a dresser and a chair. It was, instead, a place of glossy white enamel, of flush-fronted, built-in cabinets, a built-in-a-niche bed, and a cozy sitting corner. My room was isolated on the fourth floor of a conventional gray-granite low-stoop house, an altitude to which my father never and my mother rarely climbed. It was in no danger of observation, which left me free to push furniture about to achieve an interior that was not as Hoffmann would have designed it, but it made the maids giggle.

All English-type private houses in New York had the same general layout. A wide stairway from the entrance hall wound up through the center well of the house to a stained-glass skylight five stories above, while a narrow spiral back staircase wound up the back of the house from the kitchen to the fourth floor. It was connected with the front stairs by a long passage on my floor that narrowed my bedroom and created a chamfered wall through which the bedroom door was cut at the head of the front stairs. There was a narrow door from my bathroom into the passage. By locking the main bedroom door and hammering an old drapery over it on the bedroom side, I created a space that would not necessarily have inspired J. Hoffmann, but it was the best I could do in the way of a niche. The maids helped me put Edward's and my low brass footboards on my bedspring and the two high headboards on his. He thought it wildly funny when he came home for weekends and made references to prison bars or sang "She's only a bird in a gilded cage."

My bed, with the two low ends pushed back against the draped door in the diagonal wall, came as close as I could get to a Hoffmann look. For the rest we hid the chiffonier and the dresser in the dressing room closets, where there were difficulties in pulling out drawers. For the final touch of beauty that every room needs, I contrived a sitting corner by placing a discarded brown leather screen around the window, thereby shutting out all daylight; behind it I arranged a cut-down chair, some pillows and a reading lamp hooked up to the chandelier. Christmas loved it.

All of this gave the room the spacious look I was after. The wall treatments, pictures, mostly of dogs, cut out of *National Geographic Magazine* and pinned on the screen in vertical strips, made what I thought was an emphatic and pleasing accent. Accessories were a Japanese garden with sprouting horseradish-root islands, two small green turtles in a low bowl that they frequently climbed out of, some pillow rejects from downstairs and a wicker magazine rack. I went in and out through the bathroom into the backstairs passage, or through the dressing room into Edward's room and so to the front stairs. Presumably the maids told Mother what was going on upstairs, and she must have talked it over with Father. It was before the days of psychiatric consultations and their decision was apparently to do nothing and await developments. In any case nothing was said and my decorative arrangements remained undisturbed.

Unexpected encounters often lead to instant friendships and, in my case, to Vienna and Hoffmann. I awoke one night in my diagonal bed to find a many-chinned fat man in white tie and tails sitting on its foot, chuckling. He had wandered upstairs from one of my parents' endless dinner parties in search of air or a john and had found, after working his way through a labyrinth of back doors and byways, a strange room with a child asleep in gloves and hat. When I produced and aimed the water pistol, he said *"Jeessuss"* and shook the whole room with his laughter. He stayed to look at everything, the bedoodled books, the vampirish costume sketches, a plan for the further decoration of my room, which still needed a blue velvet pillow with long tassels in front of the gas logs and a white china cat to sit on it. He

■ My "Ur-Wiener" mentor, Joseph Urban, on the Lido

studied all my preparations for instant departure in the morning and gave special attention to the wall treatments. The only thing he said was *"I' bin das Urban Pepperl"*—"I am Pepperl Urban"—and went downstairs to tell my parents that they had *ein begabtes Kind*, a talented child. But with touching understanding he did not add "and a fully dressed one."

Urban was a piece of Vienna, *ein Stück von Wien*, transplanted to do settings for the Boston Opera Company in 1917 and from there to the Metropolitan Opera in New York in 1918. How that mid-war Atlantic voyage, presumably in an outsize life belt, was effected is a mystery. Pepperl always said that it was the Boston Mafia who did it, being opera lovers at heart. He had brought over his wife and two daughters, but they were in Boston and a separation was underway. I remember the first time he came to dinner, Mother put a place card on his right that read JOSEPH URBAN'S INTENDED. Those were the days of well-bred words like *expecting*, which meant a baby; an *intended* was a fiancée; and *promised, committed* or *pledged* all meant something on the order of being engaged. I didn't understand any of it, but Mother explained that Mr. Urban was planning to marry Mary Porter Beegle, whom I had seen during my ungraded period at school leaping about in brown satin bloomers. I think she taught eurythmic something or other. When I saw her from over the bannister, she was swathed in brilliant lamé with sables around the knees, very handsome and, since she could not speak German and Urban could only

27

say *Jeessuss* in English, their *intendedness* seemed to be a very happy one.

Urban did opera settings that took Boston and New York by storm with his right hand, while he revolutionized and glorified the American Girl for Flo Ziegfeld's Follies with his left. He opened his own scenic studio in Yonkers, turned a typical Grover Cleveland–type white-shingled Yonkers residence on Hudson Terrace into a startling combination of the turn-of-the-century Viennese Workshop, the Wiener Werkstätte, overlapping with discards from the Marion Davies films he did for W. R. Hearst and bits and pieces from Germany's misnamed *Jugendstil*, youth style. He worked in his architectural office in New York, did the films from an uptown studio and found still a third hand with which he guided me straight back to his own beloved Vienna and into his friend Josef Hoffmann's school, taking several years to do it.

There is a name for words that sound like what they mean, and the term *Ur Wiener*, pronounced "oor," suited Urban much better than to say he was the primordial Viennese, irresistibly charming, *gemütlich*, kind and funny. He had the ability to laugh until he shook, to chuckle until he vibrated, to infect everyone else with his humor and never with malice or venom. For me he became the prototype of Vienna, of architects and designers, and of Hoffmann.

In the fall of 1918, when I was ten years old, I was again in a new kind of latter-day ungraded class in the Blessed Sacrament Convent School in New York, where the Sisters

28

let us advance as we were able. They were so unconventional in matters of promotion that I sat among the juniors in geography, zoology and plane geometry, with the seniors in church history, but in first grade with the youngest in math and singing. We each found our own level regardless of age and size, which made for uncompetitive harmony. The Sisters were gentle. We backed out of classrooms, clutching our books and black cotton veils—which we wore just in case we felt the urge to stop in Chapel—at the same time making a curtsy worthy of the Court of St. James's while we managed to dip two fingers into the little holy water founts at the doors and make the sign of the cross without dropping anything.

At noon we ate jelly sandwiches and drank cocoa standing rigidly at a table and foxtrotted around a bare back room for fifteen minutes for our exercise. The Sisters looked on benignly, and we only came upon their unbending and resolute characters when it had to do with the saving of our souls. Those were to be kept white and blameless for as long as possible, at least until after graduation.

Once during that winter, Father and I went to the theater together when Mother had a sudden cold and no better substitute could be found. In the intermission, thinking the subject safe and sufficiently remote, he asked me quite casually what I thought I wanted to do when I grew up. He hoped I was going to say, "Be a wine-taster," but my answer had been ready and waiting for years. "I want to go to

Vienna and study design with Josef Hoffmann." In the second intermission, having calculated that there were five more comfortable years of Blessed Sacrament ahead in which I would change my mind, and secure in parental underestimation of his child, he agreed easily, but stipulated that I had to graduate from school before I could leave.

Blessed Sacrament was the perfect school for my purposes. Our Mother Superior, Sister Dionysia, who always put off until tomorrow, in heaven, what she should have done today in New York, did not recognize a major cram when she was up against one. She attributed the lightning climb of one of her duller pupils to faith and prayer. If one of her girls was ready to graduate at thirteen, that could only come from heaven, and who was she to question His will? She did not know that I was the child of a father who remembered every telephone number he had ever called and could recite *Faust* from beginning to endless end. In any case she made an appointment to talk the whole thing over with Mother in heaven. As graduation came in sight, Father wavered and wanted to postpone, but Urban prodded him on until he relented. Father and Christmas were to be grass widowers together, an unpromising arrangement, being waited on hand and foot by cook, maids and laundress, while Mother and I were to sail for Vienna.

I pulled the shelf of my steamer trunk, out of which I had been living for months, from under my bed and added finishing touches to my somewhat crushed wardrobe. There was a shoebox-sized Victrola that unfolded in such a way that one could wind it by hand, and two records, "Japanese Sandman" and "Dardanella." I also had my good-bye present from Edward, a flat camera that opened like a drawbridge in front, telescoped out on a track like an accordion and, after several adjustments, was to take snapshots of my adventures.

Someone once told me, nastily, that I was *insecure* because I tended to hamster, and I still do. For that trip I half filled an old suitcase with Kodak film and the other half with rolls of peppermint Life Savers so that I could always smell like a dentist. Both Mother and I had bottle cases in which bottles stood upright along the sides and damp sponges filled the centers. Mark Cross made special luggage for everything, but Father drew the line at traveling bookcases and we carried our Baedekers, Vernon Lee and my Dante under our arms. To travel light has since become an art, but traveling heavily was then a matter of pride and one had oneself photographed sitting on mountains of luggage; one spoke of one's twenty-odd cases and counted them ostentatiously on piers and station platforms. Cars had railings around the top and cavities for spare tires and swayed about under alps of luggage. It was long before our day of hand carts, and thick-set porters with straps and groans carried our baggage, including my tea basket with a container of alcohol for the lamp (which soaked into the tea and sugar). I also traveled with flashlight and batteries, the remains of fruit baskets from Robert Day Dean and Park and Tilford, a diary with lock and key, as well as my autograph album.

It is bound in now-faded soft purple leather, gold-embossed with the word AUTOGRAPHS. The first entry starts with a bar of music over Johann Strauss's name (it really is the opening bar of the *Blue Danube Waltz*) under which Artur Bodanzky wrote *"Glück auf* for your trip to poor old Vienna."* At the bottom of the page, Ada E. Bodanzky signed in green ink. On the next page is a brilliant little water color of a dramatic eagle clawing a helpless man. Next to it Pepperl wrote *"Glückliche Reise und hüte Dich vor Raub-vögeln!! Dein alter Joseph Urban,"* "Good voyage and beware of birds of prey, your old J.U." Then followed Clarence Whitehill, who later sang at my wedding, and L. (Leopold) Auer with a bar of the *Andante Romance*. He misspelled my name as Lilian and signed his entry in "Sincere Sympathy." After that, I was apparently on the S.S. *Arabic* on March 22 as my "fellow passenger" E. Phillips Oppenheim signed without music. The next five pages are signed in Vienna by Alfred Piccaver, Maria Jeritza, F. Schalk (director of the Vienna Opera), a stupendous scrawl by the Secessionist sculptor Anton Hanak and another bar of unrecognizable music signed by Bruno Walter. Hidden in the back, modest, undated but treasured, is the simple signature of Josef Hoff-mann. My parents were celebrity collectors (mostly musical), and the Gericke home was overrun with Vienna's great, but my autograph collection stopped with Josef Hoffmann. I seem not to have had my heart in collecting signatures, but those I have remind me of E. Phillips Oppenheim counting so many laps per mile around the *Arabic's* deck and

■ Maria Jeritza, who was to become my
daughter's godmother, here looking like
the great diva she was

■ ■

Maria Jeritza singing the "Vissi d'Arte" on her stomach at the Met.

Father, the escapist, expected us to wave at him from piers and platforms several times each year, but when we finally sailed on the S.S. *Arabic,* he managed to be on a business trip in Ohio. However, he left instructions for flowers that were delivered to us each day on board and at every Mediterranean port. I dreaded his letters, lest he had dreamed up a whole new course of study, or, for all I knew, a new set of teachers for me.

CHAPTER 3

A Lion
Remembered

Curiously, my recollections of the S.S. *Arabic*, Madeira, Gibraltar, the Mediterranean ports and Egypt coincided exactly with the snapshots I took with my new camera. There was even a picture of Mrs. Easton, who joined us at the last minute, and myself high on camels and Mother low on a donkey (taken by our dragoman) in exactly the spot in front of the Sphinx where everyone we knew had been snapped. I cannot remember what we did between pictures since my mind was apparently cemented on Vienna.

It was not *Eine Reise ins Bläue*, a trip into the blue, for me. We had been in Vienna for a long time in 1914, where I had fallen in love with a kindly lion and his cat. Children's earliest memories are intermittent, but as I look back on mine they were based either on moments of resentment or on animals. I remember that we were in London that spring of 1914 because my brother Edward was allowed to sleep in a grown-up bed in Fräulein Martha's hotel room whereas I was made to sleep in a cagelike baby bed that was wheeled into a corner of Mother's room. I do not remember anything about the assassination of the Archduke Franz Ferdinand and his wife, the Duchess Sophie, in Sarajevo, but I do remember sitting in our hotel room watching the window for a bird to come flying through the air with a message in its beak from Father in New York, which was how Mother explained the cable we were waiting for. The message when it came was just a slip of yellow paper brought to the door by a bellhop and no bird at all.

Childish memories being differently highlighted than those of adults, the bird that never came flying from New York to London is much clearer in my mind today than anything about the act that provoked World War I. The cable must have reassured Mother, for we met Father in Le Havre, where he disembarked with a car and Edward Lawrence, the chauffeur. All memories of the six of us driving across Europe were eclipsed in Venice by finding water and black gondolas in the streets and feeding corn to masses of hungry pigeons.

Whether our upbringing was my parents' invention or whether it was left over from their own recollections of being brought up in Austria, it was entirely different from that of our young American friends, who ate jelly beans, Huyler's chocolates and ice cream, while we were made to taste sophisticated foods and famous vintages. In my father's book the education of a palate could not begin too soon. My first experience with an Italian shellfish was a *Langouste* I was given on the Lido with a nip of the proper wine, and within a day I was laid low in Cortina d'Ampezzo with what they called *Ptomaina* and the trip had to be interrupted. The situation was apparently so serious that I was promised a dog if I took my bitter medicine and got well. I wanted a dog so badly that I recovered and we drove on to Trient, now Trento. The promised dog turned out to be the red cocker spaniel, who came on—and was accordingly named—Christmas, or Chris. He piddled on Mother's dark brown Lucille gown, as she handed him to me, and stayed in trouble ever after to a fat old age. He was my *Sorgenkind*, my worry child, since he built monuments where Father was bound to step, tore trouser legs and ate hats. I lived in the constant threat that *Chris must go*. He was the sort of dog that went into hysterical convulsions over every homecoming, even after a ten-minute absence.

Music to my parents was a serious business that had to be listened to whenever possible. They left the Trient hotel to attend a concert in the Piazza Dante, and after our supper we walked over with Fräulein to call for them. We stood for a time behind the seated audience, and I can still see the towering statue of Dante standing before us with hand upraised against the sky. The music stopped suddenly; there was a roll of drums and an announcement was made. They told me afterward that Austria had declared war on Serbia; it must have been the eighteenth of July, 1914.

I was old enough to feel awed, but young enough to think that the ominous Italian voice which resounded across the Piazza had been Dante's. Everyone started frantic arrangements, but Father felt secure with his American citizenship, and, forgetting that he had been an officer in the Austrian Emperor's Regiment from which he had never formally resigned and which was even then marching on Serbia, we took a leisurely and devious way north through the mountains. Much of it was done driving backwards, around hairpin curves, since, I was later told, the gas pump was not up to the Dolomites. The fact that we were traveling backwards in an American Stevens-Duryea car with an American chauffeur and French license plates because he had landed at Le Havre did not enter Father's head as a complication.

In Innsbruck, Fräulein was sent off to vacation with her family near Düsseldorf, and we did not see her again until she finally reached New York late in winter, in her large straw hat. We went on toward Vienna on the wrong side of the road, because Father was above such details and Edward Lawrence did not know that we were in the state of Salzburg, until we collided with a small car in Lofer, near Salzburg. Father, it turned out, was traveling without documents of any kind except for the car papers in French, issued in Le Havre. For Lofer that was enough; the two local gendarmes rescued him from pitchforked farmers and took him off to jail, where he denied being a French spy and maintained that he was an Austrian officer. The mayor of Lofer insisted that if he was indeed an Austrian officer he was a deserter, and whether spy or deserter, both crimes were punishable by death, which he was eager to administer for his promotion. To make matters worse the officer we had collided with was legitimately hurrying toward his regiment, whereas, the mayor pointed out, Father was hurring away from his.

During the—for us—carefree and father-free weeks that

followed, we saw nothing of Mother, who was busy having the death sentence postponed, while the chauffeur was working at putting the car together again in some blacksmith's shop. Edward and I were free at last in the Hotel Post in Lofer, with a barnyard full of fat animals and a *Sachertorte* in the kitchen once a week. Edward witnessed, turning white, the slaughtering of a pig, and I stood for hours watching sausages being filled and tied off.

An uncle of Father's, who was busy with war arrangements, finally drove down from Vienna one night to effect his release. He stayed only long enough to call the mayor a *Dummkopf*, a dolt. Father was put under room arrest until our papers arrived and when the car was repaired we started for Vienna, stopping at every small-town pharmacy to empty their bottles of benzine cleaning fluid into our gas tank. We limped into Vienna, where we swung along the Ring to converge with a bicycle rider coming out of the Währinger Strasse next to the Votive Church. The car was a Landaulet, and Mother sat in the back corner holding, as was proper on a clear day, her parasol. In an instant she leaned far out and hooked the bicycle rider under his arm with the crook of her parasol, and saved him from getting under the wheel. I remember that there were no rooms available anywhere except at the Regina, which was far below Father's standard. The chauffeur, unlike my father, traveled with identifying papers and could leave for home; the car was put in storage and we settled down to wait for the documents that would get us back to New York. I later visited the car, stored in the barn of a corset manufacturer for unknown reasons, and when I still later had a staggering offer for it, corsets had gone out of style and the car and manufacturer had disappeared.

Now that I think back on those fall weeks in Vienna, I think that Father must have been short of cash; he traveled with a letter-of-credit, but whether it was honored I do not know. We lived modestly, and even I could tell that all that out-of-door exercise was not his usual way of life. When the weather was poor, we heard concerts, visited galleries and artists' studios, and collected small objects that could be carried in our luggage. I still have an *Alt Wien* teacup with its little underglaze beehive, the cup no higher than its deep saucer, and, in spite of its weight, a ruby-red Bohemian goblet in which I now keep my pencils. Mother discovered the Wiener Werkstätte, the WW, on the Graben and came home with a little silver pillbox with, I now discover, my professor's "H" inscribed in a small square on the back. A soap bubble made of his glass did not reach New York in one piece, but I still have a rather tattered book of Grimm's *Märchen*, fairy tales, illustrated by Professor H. Lefler and Architect J. Urban, with a mermaid in a moat and Rapunzel letting down oodles of bright orange hair. We spent torturous hours waiting while Father placed orders, probably never fulfilled, in wine and gourmet shops, and was fitted for an overcoat. I remember Demel am Kohlmarkt, where Edward had *Gefrorenes*, ice cream, and to provide us with entertainment we were taken to a *Flohtheater*, flea theater, in the Prater. The fleas, hopping about wired to pink tutus, were a great disappointment. I had expected rather more Shakespearean fleas.

Years later I was reminded of that stay in Vienna when a friend brought back moving-picture films from what had been an eventless and costly African expedition graduation present. After the films were developed, she discovered that while she was photographing the expedition wives, who were seen from the back doing their laundry, an enormous lion had been present. I saw the film, and there was the lion slashing about with his tail, crouching across from the laundresses, ready to spring. He was apparently so perplexed by their carefree laughter, and by scenting no fear, that he departed. They didn't even know that they had missed the only exciting moment of the expedition.

So I too met my lion in Vienna without knowing it and missed the most exciting moment of my childhood. He was a bearded man in one of the studios we visited. His voice was vibrant, his eyes sparkled, he had great vitality and three puffs of dark hair, one in the center of his forehead and one over each ear. He was very kind and, it seemed to me, absolutely divine. I thought of him as very large and beautiful, and am now dismayed to think that he probably seemed very large because I was very small and because he wore a voluminous smock. But he was beautiful; I was confirmed in this memory when I saw the drawing that Schiele made of him on his deathbed. It was an extraordinarily beautiful face with the same chiseled quality he gave his models.

I was not allowed to touch anything, but I was allowed to look. There was a glorious painting on an easel and others glittered from the walls, but the thing that impressed me most was his tentlike smock and the discovery, due to my small size, that his legs were bare under it. It only takes an instant to become a child's unforgettable ideal; he was not only marvelous, but he had a large and handsome cat.

My parents were enchanted with a drawing of a young woman holding a shawl together under her chin. She looked so exactly like my mother that I thought for years that she had sat for it. Some sort of transaction must have taken place, for Mother took the drawing with her and gave it to me many years later. It always hung on the wall of my room wherever I went, a pencil drawing on one quarter of a sheet of *Packpapier*, wrapping paper, simply signed "Gustav Klimt."

The whole Viennese stay was a matter of leading our parents' lives with them while previously our governess had led her life with us. It was less fun; we sat through hours of adult war-talking, but it stayed in my memory as playing games in the park never would have. Father was not one to change

Gustav Klimt, in one of his self-designed smocks, ▪
holding his wonderful cat

the way he led his life, so we tagged along through Vienna's museums and galleries, artists' studios and delicatessen stores, wine merchants and the Wiener Werkstätte. We heard endless concerts, sat on hard restaurant chairs, ate what was put on our plates and were constantly on the alert for the fleas and bedbugs which Father was convinced that the war was bringing to Vienna.

For months after we docked in New York, Father dined out, and in, on his stories of waiting for our passports in Vienna without ever mentioning the fleas in pink tutus, Gustav Klimt or Klimt's cat.

CHAPTER 4

The
Secessions

Long before Mother and I embarked for Vienna, things had been going on there of which I was unaware and in which J. Hoffmann and G. Klimt played the leads. It was called the Secession, and from what I heard later the manner in which the seceders chose to secede was even worse than their actual departure from the staid Künstlerhaus, the Artists Association. It was both sensational and unforgivable, but what made it worse was that in the eyes of some it was extremely funny.

The foundation of discontent that led to the Secession seems to have gone as far back as December 2, 1848, when the Emperor Ferdinand I abdicated the throne of the Habsburg Monarchy in favor of his nephew, the eighteen-year-old Franz Joseph. Its capital city, Vienna, which was then in revolution, was a conglomeration of Gothic, Baroque, miscellany and Biedermeier squeezed into less than two square kilometers within a fortified wall. The wall, supported by nine bastions and built with the ransom money paid by the English people for the release of their King Richard the Lion-Hearted in 1192 (the second installment was never

45

paid) was surrounded by an unusually wide glacis that had originally been designed for the easier spotting of approaching Turkish invaders. As it turned out, it subsequently provided the Ottoman hordes with an opportune and comfortable tenting ground while they beleaguered Vienna. In more peaceful Biedermeier times, the Glacis became a place for colony gardens, grazing sheep and visits to Georg Kolschitzski's first Viennese coffee house, built near the spot where the routed Turkish armies had abandoned their coffee beans in 1683. Beyond the glacis lay a few princely palaces in their parks, royal stables, the Karlskirche and the nine scattered villages that had gradually grown into the first *Aussere Bezirke*, or Outer Districts.

In contrast to the other European capitals, Vienna clung to its ancient fortifications and isolationist layout and to a typical policy of procrastination and no change until after the middle of the nineteenth century. When the young Kaiser Franz Joseph I was finally persuaded that the Turks were not coming back and that something had to be done about Vienna's congestion, he looked around for room to expand into and decided that the walls had to come down. At that point every architect and artist on the Continent started to sharpen his pencils, to pull strings and advance on Vienna.

The authorization to raze the ramparts and level the bastions of Vienna and unify the Inner City with the Outer Districts was written in Franz Joseph's own hand and dated November 20, 1857. It marked the end of an era, later referred to as *Die Schöne Alte Zeit*, the Beautiful Old Time, and initiated a building revolution and a gigantic upheaval that rocked the city and forged its way into the 1890s. It also started counterrevolutions that finally exploded into Vienna's Secession and swept past the turn of the century, which the Viennese with their passion for composite or foreign words called *Jahrhundertwende*, or *Fin-de-Siècle*, which underlay the architecture and design of the twentieth century.

Franz Joseph's decision created a gigantic and concurrent space that had to be solved. It was not a collection of isolated building sites, but an enormous leveled circle around Vienna's Inner City and an open competition that attracted, challenged and inspired architects and artists from all corners of Europe. It gave new prestige to their professions and set in motion a building rage and a renewed interest in re-creating the traditional styles of the past, Greek, Roman, Gothic, Renaissance, Baroque, and every other period except what was then the present; this headed, as it was bound to, toward a clash between the past and the future, between Neo-Classicism, Neo-Gothic, Baroque, German *Jugendstil*, the nineteenth and twentieth centuries, and Vienna's own Secession versus Vienna.

The wide leveled belt that the demolition of the wall laid bare was immediately called *Der Ring* or *Die Ringstrasse* by all Viennese, long before it was officially so christened. It circled the city and connected the immense new structures with the new parks and plazas, the monuments and foun-

47

tains that now stood on what had once been the Glacis. The projects were largely unrelated revivals, palatial and sumptuously embellished, and quite naturally a *Ringstrassenstil*, a Ring Street Style, developed. It was a lifestyle as well as an epigonic architectural hodgepodge that was more reminiscent of the opulence of the 1870s than the demands of the approaching century. Caryatids and cupids, masks and shells were much in demand; banks of bays ensured all the new apartment dwellers their split-level Turkish corners and a good view of life on the street below. With the exception of Otto Wagner and Joseph Maria Olbrich, who were involved in the latter part of the *Stadtbahn Projekt*, the city railroad project, none of the gifted young architects who had watched the expansion and change around them had a hand in creating it.

Vienna's building explosion and the resultant *Ringstrassenstil* only reflected the past and negated the future; it rested in the ultraconservative hands of the establishment's *Künstlerhaus*, which looked steadfastly backwards and repeated itself from annual exhibition to annual exhibition without progress. They called their re-reproductions of the past *Historismus*, historicism, and were content that it could go on forever while they rejected all the works submitted for exhibition by the younger members. Their stodginess inflamed young Hoffmann and the reactionaries around him, who, feeling themselves neglected, unshown, unrecognized and suppressed, finally bestirred themselves from endless and futile coffee-house discussions into concerted action.

48

On the morning of April 3, 1897, some fifty-one of the *Künstlerhaus*'s most prominent younger members seceded more or less in a body, causing an uproar in academic circles that did not subside for years. Leaders of the young renegades were the men who later became my professor, the then twenty-six-year-old Josef Hoffmann, and the popular painter Gustav Klimt, who became the Secession's first president. Klimt, while still in his twenties, had won distinguished recognition for conventional murals in the *Burgtheater*, or Court Theater, and in the new Art History Museum. He had also won the desired Emperor's Prize and should have been content, but the depth of his dissatisfaction with the rule of the *Künstlerhaus* group could only be appreciated after his complete change of style and his exuberant departure from conformity could be seen at the Secession's subsequent exhibitions.

The bolters were strongly supported but not joined until the following year by Vienna's towering architect Professor *Oberbaurat* Otto Wagner, who, the offended Viennese maintained, was old enough to know better. The worst offense of all was the way the seceders went about seceding: they announced their desertion in all the Vienna newspapers on the same morning that they informed the *Künstlerhaus*, thus leaving that august body without time to resort to one of its usual delaying tactics, for example, prolonged discussions, meetings, hindrances, postponements and mollifications.

The seceders met on June 21, 1897, and decided to call

themselves the Union of Creative Artists of Austria, or the Secession. What the Artists Association called them ranged from revolutionaries to rebels, from renegades to rats and any other derogatory names they could think of. The revolters formally elected Gustav Klimt as their first president and determined on a periodical to be called *Ver Sacrum*, or Sacred Spring. But the first order of business was to design and build themselves an exhibition space where the work of the Secessionists as well as that of international artists could be shown. The *Künstlerhaus* was left to boil in its own showrooms. Being prevented from exhibiting by the "stuffed shirts" of the Artists Association and disagreements on Art versus Commerce had been the reason for the Secession, and a first show was quickly arranged in temporary quarters of the Garden Building Association on the Ringstrasse in 1898, before the Secessionists' own building was completed.

The Secessionists' first exhibition, which was arranged by Josef Hoffmann, opened the following March, 1898, took Vienna's breath away and was an immediate sensational success, even financially, which was considered mercantile and vulgar by the old school but helped to finance the Secession's contentious building. The new *Ringstrassen* society, which included wealthy industrialists and bankers, was buying contemporary paintings, while the nobility were polishing up their old masters, and nothing was more desirable in certain worldly circles than a portrait of Mamma by Klimt or an empty interior by Hoffmann. There was loud grievance and gnashing of teeth at the *Künstlerhaus*.

Most remarkable of all was the presence of Emperor Franz Joseph I at the Secession's opening, although his taste in paintings was presumably still for the rich flesh tones and the flamboyant panoramas of Klimt's teacher Hans Makart, 1840–1884, for whom the Makart Epoch was named. It was said that the Emperor stared fixedly at a painting for a long time and supposedly said *"Ah-ha, grün,"* or "Ah-ha, green." More than 53,000 people visited the show and sales netted more than 83,000 Gulden.

Many of the *Künstlerhaus*'s defectors were members of a small art group, *Der Siebener Klub*, the Club of the Seven, which met every Saturday evening at the still existing and restored Café Sperl to discuss architecture, to fume and to lay their plans. (It was their habit to stay in touch with each other with self-made picture postal cards, a practice that most of them continued into their professional lives, which led to the famous collection of postal cards, including those by Klimt, Oskar Kokoschka, Hoffmann, Bertold Löffler and Kolo Moser, that is being reproduced in part today.) Among its members was the architect Joseph Maria Olbrich, 1867–1908, three years older than Hoffmann and his close friend, both of whom Otto Wagner inherited when he took over Baron Carl von Hasenauer's class at the Academy. Another member of the Club of the Seven was supposedly Joseph Urban, the "Pepperl" who later became the successful New York architect and stage designer who sent me to Vienna to study with Hoffmann.

The new Secessionists commissioned Olbrich to design

their headquarters and exhibition building, which was to stand on the Getreidemarkt, facing the Karlsplatz on a small triangle of land donated by the Crown. All members pitched in and worked without remuneration. Known as *Die Secession*, the building was completed in 1898 and was the first building in Vienna to set a speed record. Nothing in Austria had been designed and executed in less than several years, least of all what the Viennese loudly claimed was an eyesore, and that in the very shadow of the backside of the venerable Fine Arts Academy.

There was not a Viennese, and few Austrians, who had not managed to drive past or stand around the Secession's building site to hoot and jeer while they watched it grow. They criticized it while it was still a hole in the ground and long before they could see anything to find fault with. When the flat roof was crowned with an open trelliswork cupola of 3,000 golden laurel leaves, not to mention countless berries, above a windowless white facade with sparse golden ornamentation and lettering, Viennese voices were raised in screams of derision and dissent. They called it *Das Grab des Mahdi*, The Tomb of the Mohammedan Redeemer, or a cross between a conservatory and a furnace. There is a drawing in existence that shows the Emperor Franz Joseph being received by a group of the foremost Secessionists in tails, holding their *Zylinder*, their silk hats, at the opening of the Secession's second exhibition and of their new building. The inscription on the cornice above the entrance portal reads DER ZEIT IHRE KUNST, DER KUNST IHRE FREIHEIT, to the age its art, to art its freedom—a tenet chosen by the members, which seems to have satisfied their wish for freedom and inspired them to new inventiveness and fertility of design.

There were those in Vienna who were still ridiculing the Secession when I arrived more than twenty years later, but there wasn't a Viennese who would miss an exhibition or a lecture or any other happening that took place there, least of all the sensational annual Secession Ball. (Many years later it was still an Event and I can remember feeling well dressed in what I thought was a devastating spring-green velvet dress with a train on each side, with loops for gathering them up while dancing. The trains were lined with gold lamé, and the waistline was well below my bottom— what the Viennese unashamedly called the *Popo*. Following the custom of the day, I wore shoulder-length white kid gloves and carried an enormous purple ostrich-feather fan, which was used at intervals to clear the air. We watched Ludwig Jungnickel draw caricatures of his brother artists that were projected on a huge screen while he drew. Every now and then he started to draw what looked like a fellow Secessionist and then turned it into one of his beguiling Jungnickel animals.)

Vienna was a city that had rounded the turn of the century with a new face and a new attitude. Its *Ringstrassenstil* had never been so much an architectural style as a regrouping of Grecian temples, Roman arches and Baroque angels, all finally topped off by that crowning golden touch, the Seces-

53

sion, whose liberated members were even then creating a new look that was defined as *Der Secessionstil*. It was a square-cut, rectilinear, strong simplification, a dropping of traditional ornamentation, of all historicism in contrast to the flowing lines and intertwisted lily pads of the *Jugendstil* and *Art Nouveau*. If the Secessionists leaned toward any trend, it was toward England's Arts and Crafts movement and Charles Rennie Mackintosh, whom they showed successfully in 1900. In 1903 Hoffmann rearranged the Secession to accommodate Klimt's one-man show at which eighty startlingly ornamental and resounding canvases took Vienna by storm. A year later, in 1904, Hoffmann did it again, taking the entire Secession apart to hang the enormous decorative paintings of his Swiss friend Ferdinand Hodler.

But seceding gets into the blood, and in 1905 many of the Secessionists, led by Gustav Klimt and called the Klimt Group, which included Hoffmann, Karl Moll, Moser and Wagner, seceded from the Secession in a body after bitter disagreements between those members who leaned toward Impressionism and those who defended the stylistic way of painting. The loss of the Klimt Group marked the end of the first glamour years of the Austrian Secession, although it still boasted a brilliant array of members.

I was such a convinced Josef Hoffmannite, a defender of the Secession and his Wiener Werkstätte even during the years before I actually saw them, that I always felt personally offended when I found Hoffmann listed among the *Jugend-*

stiler. He was not a follower of a German movement but the leader of two Viennese groups. For those of us who were there in Vienna, studying art, reading the German art publications and hearing the discussions, the origins and trends of the many new *Stile*, which had sorted themselves out by the 1920s, seemed clear and defined. We felt we understood the differences between the beginnings and names of the Secession and the *Jugendstil* in spite of conflicting reports from authorities on the subject. The name *Jugend*, youth, was not chosen to designate it as a young style; instead it was taken from the Munich magazine *Die Jugend*, which was founded in 1896 and edited for the first few years by the recognized German painter, illustrator, graphic artist, and book and type designer Otto Eckmann, 1865–1902. He also designed the lovely flat fat number seven that centered the brick-red cover of *Die Woche*, The Week, which was always sent up to our room so that we could look at the pictures and have suitable stories in the *Hansl-und-Gretl Stil* read to us.

Die Jugend was a satirical magazine, modeled on and rivaling the Berliners' *Pan*, which was the first time that a clear trend, a look, emerged between two covers; just to open *Jugend* was to see what was happening. The pages were illuminated, or edged, with a curiously interwoven decoration, flat and floral, a swaying of lines and tracery that often depicted stylized flowers, frequently tulips and lilies; lettering and covers were flat and ornamental, and had great appeal for the young and progressive. The actual founder of *Jugend* was the Belgian master architect, interior designer and applied artist Henry van der Velde, 1863–1957, who was director of the Art Institute in Weimar until 1914 and head of the Institut Supérieur d'Arts Decoratifs in Brussels for more than twenty years.

These men shaped the look of an influential weekly magazine and the type in which it was set. It was quickly adopted as a *Stil* in the late nineteenth century and bridged the passage into the twentieth century. *Jugend*'s flat, direct ornaments and the enormously decorative appeal of its style influenced home furnishings, illustration, applied art and interior decorating from 1896 to 1910, and acted as a show window for the trend that was inevitably called *Der Jugend Stil*. This style, long since written *Jugendstil*, is now attributed to youth instead of to an inspired and innovative group of designers behind a popular Munich publication. The name of this style is now changed at the frontiers; what was *Der Jugendstil* in Germany is supposed to be *Art Nouveau* in France and *Der Secessions Stil* in Austria. But the Secession was and remains a Viennese *Stil* founded as a result of the neglect and suppression of a group of gifted young men.

CHAPTER 5

Settling into Vienna

Father was a millionaire *manqué*, a man with all the allures and poses, the habits and extravagances of great wealth and executive genius. He did not have the fortune that went with these qualities, but that did not matter; he was a delegator of the first water, and he deputized magnificently. Whenever anything had to be done he knew exactly who would do it best (usually Mother), just how it should be done and when. He never sailed abroad or even went to the opera without leaving explicit directions behind for tasks that would take ten times longer than the time he was going to be away.

As soon as it had become clear to him that I was determined to study in Vienna and that I had fulfilled his condition, he commissioned "that old fool" Dugan, his office factotum, who was always so described behind his back, to order steamship tickets. They were to be for the longest way around, to widen my horizons, and for the first of March so that I would enter school, fully prepared, in September. Mother was entrusted with the mission of getting me to Vienna via, as it turned out, Cairo, which seems to have been the farthest-away place that Mr. Dugan could think of.

She was sternly charged with procuring the necessary guidebooks and seeing to it that I studied them. Upon arriving in Vienna, she was to find me a desirable foster home and a chaperone, since young girls could not live alone in hotels or pensions, nor could they walk about the streets unprotected. While she was about it, she was to ship home certain specified wines, find a German teacher to improve my written word, which was not as good as my spoken one, someone with whom I was to read the dramas of Goethe and Schiller.

Mother's friend Tante Emma Easton, who had not been able to resist coming along, thought it extremely funny that we sailed loaded down with lists, orders, memos and *aides-mémoire*, only to be met at various Mediterranean ports by messengers from Thos. Cook bearing Father's written afterthoughts and always accompanied by a bunch of flowers. He reminded us that I was to make a cold-water cure, take a course in the history of art and sit straight. Orders included dried mushrooms from Verona and Tokay from Hungary; most important, I was to learn to *draw*. Father did not hold with art that did not stand on a cast in plaster foundation.

After circling the Mediterranean, we had a lovely guidebookless tour, zigzagging north through the length of Italy in spring and ending in Venice. The last lap of our journey was on the Orient Express, which was as glamorous then as they are making it today. During all these years of dreaming about Vienna, I never once thought about its geographical location, which turned out to sit on just about the same latitude as upper Newfoundland, with winds from the Alps and the icy steppes of Russia. We shed the warmth and sunshine of Italy through various tunnels and over high passes that night and pulled into a misty and cold Vienna the next morning.

Vienna smelled, as it will always smell, of burning coke and fog, of roasting chestnuts and coffee, probably chicory, of baking bread and just a tiny whiff of lavender. The taxi was ancient, the streets bumpy and the houses grimy, but it was Vienna and I was happy.

Father's schedule had allowed time for what he called an acclimatization period. I was to adjust slowly to Vienna before I entered school and before Mother left me to return to New York. It made me feel a little like those tropical animals that are made to sit shivering on Brioni while they are being hardened for some North European zoo. From Vienna's Sudbahnhof, we went straight to the Hotel Bristol, then known as the New Bristol, where the frock-coated *Herr Direktor*'s bows and heel clickings, the cool prewar linen sheets, the silk-paneled walls, the flowers on the breakfast tray, and our red-velvet-draped and betasseled salon reduced the acclimatization from months to minutes.

As soon as we were unpacked and suitably dressed, I remember carrying a "Burnt Henna" moiré parasol; with Baedeker in hand and great expectations, we took a taxicab to see the *Schule* I had set my heart on attending. Our driver, who was almost as tottery as his car, took us the long way around Vienna's pride, the Ringstrasse, where the city walls had been demolished about sixty years before to make way for the Ringstrasse's building boom, the results of which crescendoed from one ornate (now venerable and war-worn) structure to the next. Starting with Heinrich Ferstel's Neo-Gothic Votive Church and Théophile Hansen's New-Greek Parliament, it skipped from revival to revival until there were no architectural styles left to revive. All was rich magnificence, from the two vaguely Saint Peter-ish museums, past the impressive Academy, the Opera and the New Bristol, as far as the Schwarzenberg Platz, where the *K.u.K.* (*Die Kaiserliche und Königliche*) *Ministerien*—that is to say, His Majesty the Emperor of Austria's and King of Hungary's ministries—seem to have lost interest, or possibly money. By the time the buildings reached the Stubenring, Herr von Ferstel was reduced to reviving the Italian Renaissance as London had conceived it, and designed the Austrian Museum of Applied Art to remind one vaguely of a miniature Victoria and Albert Museum without the fortresslike nuances. He added medallions bearing artists' heads, terra-cotta ornamentation, mosaics, a frieze and a fairly impressive portaled entrance, up several wide steps.

For the adjoining Applied Art School, the Kunstgewerbeschule, there was only the poor-man's-bare-palazzo look left. My *Schule* was an unemotional nothing of a three-story structure with an astylar facade of ocher-to-German-mustard-colored brick with olive-drab trim. There was an inconspicuous one-step-up doorway and a nameplate as large and impressive as the lid of a shoebox. It looked like a car barn, without the large doors, and gave a clear indication of where applied art stood in relation to the fine arts, which were housed in great splendor on the Schiller Platz.

We were both sure this bare warehouse-palazzo-barn could not possibly be our destination. I remember that we tried to urge our driver on to an impressive earlier-day Pentagon-type building that lay beyond. It had sentry boxes topped with empty helmets and double drive-in entrances, and it did, in fact, turn out to be the *Regierungs Gebäude*, the Government's Edifice. But our chauffeur would not budge; he dug in his heels, and we had to accept the *Schule* as it stood. I do not know what I had been expecting—perhaps a combination of the Strozzi Palace and, with Hoffmann always in mind, the Palais Stocklet. I had certainly expected Hoffmann to make himself felt on the outside of the building, but there was nothing. We were so disappointed that we stayed in the cab and told the driver to return to the Bristol by the shortest way. Back in our red salon, I felt the first flutter of the opening-day-of-school butterflies that lay ahead.

I put off thinking about school while the Hotel Bristol spoiled and pampered me, but the moment we left the hotel we came face to face with poverty, scars and need. Vienna after World War I was a city of people who had lived for many years in shabby apartments, in the same clothes and with only one subject of conversation: war. They had huddled in one heated room in their cold homes, and many had burned their furniture to keep that one room warm. They walked wherever they had to go and had little communication in winter, but their courage was unbroken, as was their unfailing humor. Vienna's *Genius Loci*, the bagpiper known as *Der Liebe Augustine*, had sung when he fell into the pesthole in 1679, and he was still singing when they fished him out the next morning. The Viennese were still able to joke and sing.

It was a city that awoke to a strange new double life, to its own rejuvenated past and to the progress that had taken place, mostly in *Amerika*, during the war years. Orchestras and bands turned back to their own enchanting waltzes, interrupted by the first strains of jazz, and there were women who took to the *Bubi Kopf*, bobbed hair. They went to the movies once a year, which were flickery and *stumm*, silent, and they lent each other and endlessly discussed new books, as, for example, *Hauptstrasse* by Sinclair Lewis and *Kaiser Jones* by Eugene O'Neill.

Spring came slowly to Vienna; the low mists cleared, and the chestnut trees bloomed with white and pink candles. Every now and then there was the haunting scent of a linden tree in bloom, which always held me breathing deeply until I could smell it no longer. To some, Vienna was a sad relic of the Habsburgs, but to me it was as I had dreamed it into place, and even impoverished and bereft as it was, it fulfilled that dream. There never was an instant of disappointment. The city started to come true for me; I discovered her Baroque convolutions, her Romanesque foundations and tall Gothic arches, and her simple cellar restaurants where scrambled eggs with mushrooms fresh from the woods made heavenly dinners. I learned that to eat a whole meal in one place was a lost opportunity, so we ate progressively, ending with a *Torte* at Gerstner or Demel or at some little *Konditorei* on a back street. I also found that Vienna was *journalière*, a polite French way of explaining a sort of glow, or lack of it, that makes plain women pretty on one day and beautiful women ugly on the next. Vienna was like that—*grantig*, ill-humored, on a rainy day, and full of charm and courtesy, gallantry and civilities, when the wind turned, all in three-quarter time. I never did acclimatize to Vienna; it became an instant and unbreakable addiction.

Settling into Vienna turned into a second delicious surprise settlement, namely the adjustment to Vienna's food and eating habits. Austrian cookery borrowed a little from across its borders and came up with a cuisine that I adopted with enthusiasm, especially as there were often as many as three desserts at a single meal. Viennese eating habits before the war, when the *mollige Figur*, rounded figure, was in style, had run to as many as six or seven pleasantly spaced food breaks a day. It all began with an early-bed tea, went on to a coffee or chocolate with crescents, croissants, followed by *Gabelfrühstück*, a "fork breakfast," that included something, ideally a goose-liver pâté, that had to be eaten with a fork and washed down with sherry. Dinner was often divided into two parts, going from soup to a *Mehlspeise*, a dessert that contained flour, all served in the dining room,

63

after which the diners migrated to the living room where coffee, a *Torte* and pastries, and a *crème* awaited them. The late afternoon tea was called a *Jause*, and after a concert, opera or theater there was supper, presumably at Sacher's. The Viennese kept in shape by walking, waltzing, galloping on a horse or in a ballroom, Turkish baths and corseting. When we arrived in Vienna, the Viennese were throwing themselves on everything they had missed with such gusto that I too was carried away into starting a second interest, a second love and a second career, *Food*, to go hand in hand with what Hoffmann was going to teach me.

Father continued his letters of instruction, and Mother checked each item off religiously. She found a ramrod Fräulein Rein, who was to teach me German literature; this lasted just long enough to let me read through Goethe's *Faust* before Father switched me to a German course in Shakespeare. In the meantime I wrote the essays, memorized the poems and improved my penmanship and horsemanship according to the orders in Father's letters.

The details of entry into the Kunstgewerbeschule (one can always trust the Austrians to use one word when five are needed) were arranged and I was told just recently that there must have been some sleight of hand about my application since I was five years below the entrance age. Whether this was done by Urban from New York, or whether Mother juggled or Hoffmann closed an eye, I don't know, but school's opening in early September hung over my head all that summer. I discovered that one can be immeasurably happy and scared to death at the same time, which was no wonder since I was recently shown my school application blank and discovered that all the hanky-panky had been my own. There in black on white, in my own newly developed, picturesque and Anton Hanak–like handwriting, I had filled in a birth year that was five years earlier than my own.

Mother ordered Father's favorite Tokay from the exactly specified sunny side of a wine hill in Hungary and shipped off the Wachau apricot confiture he favored. She spent days finding enormous table napkins that his dinner guests could wrap around themselves, and handkerchiefs as large as tea cloths. She also found time to compile a list of possible foster mothers and foster homes for me, and stayed on at the Bristol while I tried out the three that sounded most promising.

The first of these was a charming Russian princess, whose Vienna apartment turned out to be a small *Schloss*, crammed full of more charming Russians, located just under the Semmering, several hours from school. The second choice was right in Vienna, across the city from school, in the home of an opera fan who may or may not have been a diva in her day. She was obviously going to spend the additional income I provided on taking us both to the opera—to *stand* at the opera, as it turned out. The first afternoon we went to hear— we could not possibly see it—an uncut performance of *Die Götterdämmerung*, The Twilight of the Gods, from the topmost gallery. A long intermission was provided for dinner, but my hostess used it to sit in a vacated seat. After a dark walk home at midnight, I too went into a *Dämmerung*, and the doctor who was called said there was an emptiness of blood in the head. I moved back to the Bristol and on to my third foster home after the circulation had been restored.

My third foster home was owned by a woman who revolutionized the traditional arrangement; she loved large, uncluttered rooms and regimented all her cupboards and closets along the walls of her foyer. In Vienna the old apartment houses had all been built along uncomplicated lines. The street entry was for carriages, with a small door cut into the large one for pedestrians. From this passage or courtyard one passed the *Portier*'s lodge to a stone stair and, in the more luxurious buildings, a perilous lift that crawled up the open stairwell or up the outside of the building. The porter unlocked the lift door in return for a fee and a tip, and one always walked down. The floor plans were alike, though the decorations ranged from none to palatial. Having arrived at one's apartment floor one entered tall double doors, a foyer and a string of elegant rooms, opening into each other. The kitchen and a *Cabinet*, an almost windowless room that faced on the courtyard and the bathroom and *Clo* were hidden in the remotest and least accessible corner that could be found.

Tenants brought their own *Schränke*, closets, and every well-regulated family owned the tall clothes and linen closets, its china and glass cupboards, kitchen cabinets, storage closets and combinations. There were arrangements that had mirrored center sections with sentry-box-like ends in which long-trained evening gowns, long opera cloaks and old wedding dresses were stored. The tops of these closets were repositories for hat and storage boxes and for inches of dust; under the closets was an accumulation of old toys, the family cat, narrow corset boxes and everything a family loses through the years.

The room that had been allotted to me faced the street, and a towering Beidermeier wardrobe, right opposite the front door, was to accommodate all my hanging possessions and shoes. This left the room free for the traditional Viennese obstructions: the tile stove with its briquettes made out of pressed coal dust and sawdust, a coal scuttle, the marble-topped washstand and slop pail behind its discreet screen, an analyst's type of couch upholstered in Oriental carpeting, and a writing desk. There was also a high narrow bed with a mountainous *Feder Bett*, feather cover, a nightstand, a curio cabinet and chests of drawers, a harp or other musical instrument with a music stand and footstool. There had to be a table with an Oriental carpet cover, sometimes there was a *prie-Dieu* and heavily framed pictures that crashed from the walls now and then, predicting or causing a death in the family. No room was complete without a clothes tree and a towel rack, and various worn areas in the rugs were covered with miscellaneous carpeting over which we tripped.

I had barely installed all my clothes in the hall wardrobe when an unidentified delivery girl made off with everything in one huge armful, including the arctics. Gone was the still unworn *Wiener Werkstätte* coat with my first adult fur collar.

An unsuspected grandmother, smoking a black cigar, emerged from the *Cabinet*, but no amount of *"Das gibt's ja nicht"*— "That can't have happened"—could replace my clothes. My brand-new insurance agent, a blind ex-officer, could do nothing, and Mother bought me at Zwieback a dark blue cloth coat with an opossum collar, in which I moved back to the Bristol.

After that, Mother and I took the train to Munich, to see Milka Ternina, once the Metropolitan Opera's first Tosca, who was convinced that she knew the exactly proper and musically suitable home for me with friends from Vienna, who it just so happened were visiting her at the time. At her tea table we met Professor Wilhelm Gericke, former conductor of the Vienna Opera and founder of the Boston Symphony Orchestra, his wife, Paula, and his daughter Katharine. My future in Vienna was settled over tea, and Katharine's friend Johanna Beihl was engaged, sight unseen, to chaperone me on all nonschool occasions. I was not to be let out of her sight for a minute.

With the roof over my head and proper supervision arranged, Mother went on to Father's next commandment. I was to learn to draw properly and traditionally, starting with a cube, and the plaster cast of a hand, then on to the Laocoön Group, graduating to a draped model and finally a model with nothing on, called an *Akt* in German. I was not just to do squiggles and frivolities—none of those newfangled modern wrinkles for Father. Mother consulted a distant cousin who knew the etcher Ferdinand Schmutzer, but even he could not get me into the Academy on any score, since I was too young. The Austrians were a meticulously upright people but casual, and the simplest way they could find for me to enter the Academy was to go through the front door, up the stairs and into a room facing the Schillerplatz assigned to Professor Schmutzer and his pupils. I started immediately and drew from the cube, the cast, bits of drapery and apostle-type bearded models with Schmutzer's prize pupil Rudolf Kucera, while he in turn drew me.

I walked to the Academy from the Bristol each day during that early summer, keeping Father happy and myself in a tizzy, dreading the day when I would be confronted by a naked man plus the penetrating stares of Mr. Kucera. He was, by then, etching me directly onto a copper plate and hissing every time I moved. I also foresaw trouble when Hoffmann's school opened in September, complicated by the fact that Father had discovered that a Professor Friedrich had an evening life class for women in Vienna that he felt I should add to my fall schedule.

After a summer in Elbogen, near Karlsbad, I moved into my room at the Gerickes, at Beatrixgasse 30, in the third *Bezirk*, or district, just across the Stadtpark from school and, following my birthday in July, life began for me at fourteen.

CHAPTER 6

At Home
with the Gerickes

The Viennese, beset by enormous postwar housing short-
ages, were assigned a certain number of rooms in their own
apartments or houses, according to the size of each family.
The remaining rooms were crammed with paying guests, or
PGs, and everyone had either had a hideously appalling
experience with a PG or directly or indirectly knew someone
else who had done so. Most PGs smoked too much, tipped
too little, hung their bedding out of the windows or stole
the bric-a-brac. I remember that Mother and I went to tea
at the home of an impressive Frau Hofratin, with a Bourbon
profile, a vibrant double chin and lots of jet bangles. Her
apartment door was opened by her actor paying guest in his
underdrawers, because he was ironing his only pair of trousers in the front hall, under the portraits of her lesser ancestors and their horses. It was an especially memorable tea,
as I had not known until then that Austrian men wore Buster
Brown–style garters and long stockings. I remembered the
scene, as a warning, some years later, when all American
girls in Vienna were swamped with marriage proposals from
men, not necessarily young and not necessarily single at the
time, who saw such an alliance as preferable to waiting

endless years for a quota number with which to emigrate to *Amerika*.

Single men who had twelve-hour jobs and two pairs of trousers were more desirable PGs than single women, who were apt to keep either cats or canaries or receive someone else's (male) paying guests in their rooms, but Americans— whether male or female, old or young—were to be preferred over all others because they were *rich*. An American art student who was in school all day, rarely spoke, ate very little, did not play a musical instrument or keep a pet and paid in dollars was about as perfect as anyone could wish for, and the Gerickes were content. They sat back and looked into an assured and peaceful future. They did not dream that within no time at all their lives would be disrupted, that I would acquire an enormous Airedale puppy, that I would expect to bathe regularly in hot water, that I would go out and be seen in public places alone with single men, and that I would have fifty pairs of shoes. Actually I had about ten, it being the style in America to have one's shoes dyed to match one's dresses, but since I had no room in my wardrobe they stood in my bookcase for all to see. Showing them to friends in my absence was a disquieting experience for all and poor Mrs. Gericke said, "*Was noch?*" ("What next?").

I moved into the Gerickes' home and life in autumn, just in time to witness the first attempts on the part of the Viennese hostesses to re-create the pleasures and delicacies, the intricacies and finessings of prewar entertaining in post-

71

war circumstances. Their PGs made it possible for them to install telephones, resurrect old servants or engage new ones and to eat meat once a day. They did lose one or two spare bedrooms, but what was that in comparison to cash? And in any case most PGs were bed-and-breakfasters who did not mix into their lives. In my case the situation was different; the musical atmosphere and a daughter who painted academically appealed to Father, and the cultural and social advantages that the Gerickes proposed to provide meant that they had to have me at their table and at all the various functions that a PG's presence made possible.

Mrs. Gericke was more fortunate than her friends in that she acquired a second dollar-paying PG from Boston, a Miss Gladys Greene, who was rarely seen since she was taking singing lessons and attending concerts, but her presence was felt in extra restored luxuries in the Gericke household. The first of these was the *Friseurin*, the house hairdresser who came each morning to arrange the better Viennese hairdos. These were usually imposing pompadours held in place by a hair net and a well-balanced way of life. The point was to secure an appointment for an hour when the *Friseurin* had several calls behind her and could report on interesting doings. She was the forerunner of the morning news broadcasts and gossip columns. When Mrs. Gericke had an evening event on her schedule, the hairdresser returned and made corrections and additions, as, for example, feathers and a cloud of brilliantine. A light peignoir was worn for these opera-

■ This little silver bowl was my first purchase from the Wiener Werkstätte and it stood in my room at the Gerickes'.

tions, a popular Christmas present, and every few weeks there was a shampoo.

Mrs. Gericke's second new acquisition after Miss Greene's and my arrival was Frau Anna, a cook with aristocratic references. The apartment was scrubbed by the charwoman, Frau Toni, who had weathered the soapless war years and stayed on to enjoy her reward in American brown soap. The third innovation was an elderly and formidable waitress called Monika, who rounded out the staff. Her black skirt came down to her ankles, her high collar and apron were starched, and she rustled when she walked. She activated the musical pixie in Professor Gericke, who called her *Har-Monika*, concertina, because her high-button black shoes squeaked loudly. On other occasions he called her *Harmonika-Zug*, corridor or compartment train, when she dragged in a heavy tray, or *Mund-Harmonika*, mouth organ, when he wanted a second helping. He called her *Zieh-Harmonika*, accordion, whenever she served a pulled *Strudel* or tough meat. She was not amused by any of it.

Monika was also the ambulatory telephone operator; she answered it in the *Foyer*, went to tell Mrs. Gericke who was calling, went back for the instrument and plugged it into the outlet next to which Mrs. Gericke sat expectantly every morning, after the hairdresser and before marketing. Mrs. Gericke then went through a metamorphosis; she turned into a gushing geyser, she was capable of such alarming enthusiasms as *"Meine liebe liebste Stephanie"* or *"Geliebte Eugenie,"* *"Mein verehrter Herr Direktor,"* *"Verehrte Hofrätin."* She had only love, admiration and devotion for her telephone world. Her conversations were endless; she made ecstatic sounds and rejoiced and lived for the rest of the day on every conversation. Many Viennese had not had telephones before the war; their messages, visiting cards and invitations were delivered by the ancient red-capped *Dienst-*

74

männer, service men, and the telephone was an unending novelty. Of all the things that peace and American PGs had restored to Vienna, the morning telephone calls were the pinnacle.

Only the second half of nineteenth-century Vienna could have produced Frau Paula Gericke. She was always aware of what was *correct*, what *one did*, and she always did it correctly. She was small, bandbox neat, precise, unsmiling, and from the moment she woke until she fell asleep she was in a hurry. She ran about on small feet, a little like a pouter pigeon, and poked her fine small nose into everything. She was critical, fussy, highly musical, *gebildet*, educated, and looked sternly through her *Zwicker*, a *Pinz-nez* attached by a fine golden chain and hairpin to her pompadour. She gushed torrentially but could turn it off in a second if it was not needed. There were heart flutters at times, and one night there was great commotion, a doctor and strange sounds, when she mistakenly drank Eau de Cologne instead of Tincture of Valerian for a small palpitation of the heart. Katharine was a replica of her mother, with a sound heart and a sense of humor, and Professor Wilhelm Gericke was the object of their joint twenty-four-hour-a-day devotion. He spoke very little, played on his beautiful Bechstein concert grand for hours and never did accustom himself to the fall of the *Krone*. He carried his billfold of several hundred *Krone* notes on dignified walks, refusing to accept that it took a small satchel of bills of such denomination to buy a postage stamp.

Mrs. Gericke clung to the old just as tenaciously as Herr Professor, but she stopped to give the beggars along his route a more meaningful packet of paper bills than the worthless aluminum coins he dug out of his change purse to give them. She still clanked about the apartment with a *châtelaine* at her waist, a large and handsomely interwoven silver "PG" for Paula Gericke, *not* for paying guests, from which the keys of every cupboard in the apartment dangled. It was the sort of thing that prewar brides were given by their mothers with a sermon on the frugal management of their households. The Austrians did not have a Mrs. Beeton, but they had Maria von Rokitanzky, the socially acceptable wife of an army officer, who wrote a book by which everyone cooked divinely and stored food under lock and key. When Frau Anna had a *Sachertorte* in mind, Mrs. Gericke unlocked one of her treasure chests and measured out all that was needed, including seven eggs and a pinch of this and that. She then locked up carefully, Frau Anna retired to her kitchen and Frau Professor, with her *châtelaine* safe in her handbag, walked down to Frau Weisshappel's butcher shop on the Petersplatz to carefully control the scales while her boiling beef was being weighed.

Daily marketing in Vienna was necessary, since supplies came from the country in limited amounts, and Frau Gericke and her friends, who would not have raised a hand in lowly household tasks, set out with their string bags for the pleasure of getting the better egg and at the same time seeing what was going to be served on other tables. So the ladies went to market, bickered, traded and bartered, gossiped and sampled little slivers of cheeses. On Frau Gericke's way home, she stopped for a light *Gabelfrühstück* and a glass of sherry, which brought her home benign and rosy in time to preside over the soup tureen. Dinner, in the middle of the day, was announced by a chime that Herr Professor played with feeling, whereupon we all trooped into the dining room knowing it was going to be boiled beef, but unsure of the starches. Wilhelm and Paula Gericke sat opposite each other, and Katharine and I sat across from each other between them, with room to spare for at least four more, while Miss Greene was usually at her lessons. Monika backed into the dining room with an enormous tray, kicking the door open and shut resoundingly, swished around and plunked the tray on the side table, because her background was not as aristocratic as Frau Anna's. From there she placed the steaming soup tureen in front of Mrs. Gericke, where it barely fitted under the rim of the suspended stained-glass lamp shade that looked a little like a large inverted tea caddy by Tiffany.

Mrs. Gericke rose to her feet and ladled out the soup along with carefully selected portions of the *Einlage*, the inlay, a garnish that was placed in the center of the soup. Monika handed out the plates and everyone fell to. It was a ceremony that took place in every well-regulated Viennese home at about the same time each day, and while it may once have been celebrated with a delicate lobster bisque or a sherried pheasant consommé with pistachio quenelles, in

postwar Vienna it was always the stock in which the beef
had boiled all morning. Everyone ate their soup from the
front of their spoons with a small contented *Schlürf* and an
upward motion of the hand to impel the inlay. They tilted
their plates toward themselves to spoon up the last drop,
and they sighed with pleasure. It was heaven after years of
dried lentil and gray potato soups without inlays.

Monika backed out with the tureen and backed back in
with the sliced boiled beef surrounded by its boiled vege-
tables, which she passed to each of us. No Viennese gentleman would be seen carving at the table. They did not mix
drinks or salads or participate in any household tasks, other
than controlling the heat and, in view of Professor Gericke's
background, pinging the chimes.

In better homes in the 1920s, meat was always *Gekochtes
Rindfleisch*, boiled beef, of various ages and tenderness. I
think it was slaughtered when it was felt the end was near.
Veal was too precious to eat before it grew old, hens had to
lay eggs, and pork was for the people and their sausages.
The accompaniments and sauces that were served with the
boiled beef were as varied as the combinations that can be
made with a pack of playing cards. Frau Anna's versatility
was endless, and bread dumplings, noodles, potatoes, small
Spätzle and *Servietten Knödel* (a large dumpling cooked in
a napkin) came with *Paradeis Sosse* (tomato sauce), cu-
cumber, horseradish, caper, mushroom and dill sauces, or
with mustard, vinaigrette, egg, chive and paprika sauces.
Professor Gericke was delighted when tomato sauce coin-

cided with bread dumplings, and I waited for the day when potato dumplings came together with mushroom sauce.

Just to make absolutely sure that we had our starches, or possibly for lack of eggs, fruit and cream, dessert was usually rice, noodles, dumplings or pancakes. Frau Anna had little opportunity to demonstrate her talents, but they flowered when Bruno Walter came for his weekly lunch and when Mrs. Gericke had her re-established monthly *Jours* and bi-monthly *Quartette*. Much to my surprise, Monika also bloomed on these occasions with a second starched petticoat, or maybe a few sheets of the daily *Presse*, and a crisp white head frill that made her look like a sorrowful President Woodrow Wilson at a costume ball.

Conversation at meals was always *made*, a very different matter from just talking as we did at home. It was probably all part of the *Kultur* and polish I was to acquire. When Monika kicked in the dessert, it usually coincided with the ringing of the doorbell and the Mocha Callers called. Either Herr von Mayhofer, who had the *Atelier* at the top of the building, or someone who was within smelling distance of Frau Anna's brewing Mocha. The coffee was served in tiny cups with just a taste of the far-from-sweet sweet and some of the hand-filled cigarettes were shared. These visits were *Gemütlich*—an untranslatable word for "cozy"—and amusing, as the dropped-in guests felt obliged to bring the latest jokes and juicy bits of scandal instead of the flowers they could not afford. The coffee callers left in time for everyone to have their little naps before the *Jausen* tea guests came in. This was a modest and almost costless getting together in a city that had once entertained lavishly.

But after more than six years of privations and doing without, the Viennese hostesses were finally able to accumulate enough sugar and butter, eggs and almonds, chocolate, apricot jam and hazelnuts to bake the pastries for which each one had a secret recipe that made her salon famous. There was rum for their tea and the ancient footman, Leonhard, who had presided over every better Viennese at-home, or *Jour*, for the last forty-five years before the war, came back into circulation, more bowed and balder, with darned white cotton gloves and a greenish tailcoat that practically dragged on the floor behind him.

Mrs. Gericke was determined to be the first Viennese hostess to re-establish her monthly day *at home*, her *Jour*. It was a prearranged day on which Viennese ladies sat at home in what remained of their *best*, surrounded by their *Jour Brötchen* (small open sandwiches), their *Jour Gebäck* (miniature versions of their very best pastries), their *petits fours secs*, and received their guests. After much telephonic date bickering with rival hostesses, so that no two *Jours* would conflict, she secured the desirable First Wednesdays (of the winter months) and settled down to checking old guest lists and studying recipes. When the *Jour Kalender* was finally arranged, Mrs. Gericke wrote First Wednesdays on her visiting cards and left them on her friends to signal the great rebirth. It meant that each hostess could justify her own

■ ■

Jour's extravagance since she and her husband, in turn, could count on at least twenty hearty outside *Jours* each month. Frau Professor Gericke's first at-home was a tremendous success; every card that had been left brought a twittering guest, all of whom were curious, hungry and in their old finery.

The Viennese had gone through a great deal, which did not mean that they had mellowed or were willing to give an inch; what had been good enough for the Habsburgs was still good enough for them. They took up where they had left off because they wanted everything to be the same as they remembered it. I was the youngest and as such I had to sit on a side chair against the wall in a remote corner of the room from where I could watch the goings-on. The oldest and most honorable guest sat on the pink-gilt Louis XV *Canapé* on the right hand of her hostess. The other guests fell into place according to rank; the four most august ladies sat on faded fauteuils around a marquetry table in front of the *Canapé*, and the least distinguished sat somewhere near me on a banquette, stool or gilt chair. Everyone moved up one place when the more stately departed. Men balanced their cups of rum-laced tea while they rotated around the seated ladies; it was called circulating.

The conversation could not have been more stilted; ladies were either all nearsighted or lifted their lorgnettes to express disdain, not to help their vision. One Countess, whose cigarette I was asked to light, blew out the flame as I turned to light a Baroness's cigarette with the same match, which

81

gave me my first inkling of social stratification. Arrivals and departures, duration of stay, subjects of conversation and amount of food consumed were all more or less prescribed. Farewells were said in the salon with hand kissings, bowings and heel clickings so that guests were free and unobserved to leave tips for the *Personal*, the staff, on their way out. They also left the proper number of visiting cards, with one corner bent over, on a second tray that was provided for the purpose in the *Foyer*. After all the guests had gone, the cards were counted, checked against the List and re-arranged, with the most impressive ones on the top. The bent-over corner meant that the owner had been there in person.

The Gerickes' *Quartett* consisted of musicians selected from Professor Gericke's musical past and involved considerable entertaining. There were little teas with the first violin to discuss the program, to compose the most harmonious menu and to select the other instruments. The musicians were always spoken of as the cello or *Die Bratsche*, viola, and when Mrs. Gericke counted up her guests she invariably said, "the cello and his wife" or "*Die Bratsche* and his sister." There was always a small dinner party for the quartet and its wives after the final rehearsal and the gala dinner after the concert. Guests were selected for their social standing and their musical understanding, but the rush to the dining room after the final discreet applause indicated an epicurean appreciation as well.

It was all new to me; no one at home had so much as a duet or ever directed who was to sit where at receptions or at-homes, who was to leave first and just how many minutes a pre-dinner-invitation-thank-you call should last or what should be talked about. But Vienna was still clinging to the conventions and court etiquette that dated back to the Habsburgs, and they wanted to take up their lives exactly where they had left them off in 1914, driving in the Prater, bowing to each other on the Corso, drinking rum-laced tea at each other's *Jours* or listening to music in pink, now somewhat faded salons. Their turn-of-the-century clothes had been turned and re-turned; braid had been ripped from uniform trousers and jackets; brocaded draperies had been mended and patched. Everyone deplored the beautiful uniforms that had made men glamorous, as their shabby postwar uniforms-changed-into-suits never could. They saw each other as they remembered, charming and debonair. I could only see them as they were. Everyone had their visiting cards reprinted, complete with their abolished titles, which they crossed out in the hope that it would look as though they couldn't afford new cards and had to make do with the old ones. After a time they just drifted back into using their titles, although they were just *Herr* and *Frau* in the telephone book. Ancestors remained on the walls and crowns remained on linens, silver and porcelain. Daughters of the house were always at their mother's salons, starting at the hair-ribbon stage and ending when they had a salon of their own. Katharine celebrated her thirtieth birthday while I was there, on which occasion she was given a house key and was allowed to move about at parties, while I could be seen in the background, but could certainly not be heard. I rose when women as well as men entered the room, and stood until they were seated.

On evenings when Mrs. Gericke was not entertaining or being entertained, we ate *Eine Eierspeise*, one egg for each dish, prepared by Katharine, and sat cozily around the dining room table doing our *Handarbeit*, handiwork. Katharine worked on Christmas presents, Mrs. Gericke mended and Professor Gericke controlled the temperature. I rolled the pure *Wiener Wald* cigarettes that Mrs. Gericke was not supposed to smoke, a restful occupation as soporific in its effects as peeling mushrooms or running prayer beads through one's hands. When the room became too cold, we all went to bed. Vienna slept behind double closed windows with a weighted window pillow between, heavy draperies and a window screen. We crawled under deep featherbeds and stepped onto *Bettvorleger*, fur rugs, when we got up. The daily bath I had requested when I arrived was forgotten as the halls and passages and the place that Fräulein Martha, while still under the Monarchy, had described as "*wo der Kaiser allein hin geht*" (where the Emperor goes alone) were all unheated.

Wanting to go to the john was a problem during my school days in Vienna, as it still is in Austria today. One could not ask to go to the "bathroom," because one was then led, by a bewildered hostess, to a small inside room off a back hallway. In it there was always a complicated prewar hot-water-heating contraption up near the ceiling and an unused bathtub under a heavy wooden cover. Depending on the status of one's host and hostess, this was usually loaded with the winter's supply of conserves and pickles, bars of home-made yellow soap and an ancient wringer. An anxious look around revealed nothing more than brooms, mops and a mop bucket draped with a stiff chamois, but not a sign of a toilet.

If one asked, more properly, to be allowed to "wash one's hands," one was ushered into a bedroom where a washbowl and a pitcher of cold water were discreetly hidden behind a low screen on a marble-topped washstand. The pitcher and bowl, usually flowered, were surrounded by matching tooth mug, soap dish and shaving bowl, and further personalized by shaving and tooth brushes and a sponge bag. There was, of course, not a trace of a john.

Furthermore, the bathrooms and johns in Austria were installed in the oddest corners many years, or even centuries, after the homestead, the apartment house or the castle had originally been built. One could not rely on finding them in the usual places by instinct alone; they were never off the master bedroom, and going through one of those unmistakable small doors at the head of the stairs was apt to bring one out on the fire escape. In one case, in a castle in Tyrol, we had to cross the ramparts in midwinter with a lantern to locate the john. At the Gerickes', it was in the *Foyer*, immediately next to the front door, and the chances of going there unobserved were nil, what with guests, deliveries and Monika with the telephone.

85

To make matters worse, we never knew what to call the johns in German. "Ladies' room," translated into the *Damen Zimmer*, meant a sort of boudoir, usually pink, into which ladies retired to write their letters and loosen their stays. It could also mean the rooms that were set aside in a *Kaffeehaus* for the ladies who did not smoke and wanted to listen to music while they drank hot chocolate and ate pastries. Johann Strauss was a great drawing card in just such a ladies' room. By the same token, the *Herren Zimmer*, or men's room, was a smoking room or den.

A *Toilette* was a major evening gown for great occasions with *Décolleté* and train, while such a designation as "W.C.," pronounced "Vay Tzay," although it stemmed from Europe's first water closet, installed for Queen Victoria in Coburg, was considered vulgar. One could ask, however, for the *Clo* or *Klo*, which appears to have been another abbreviation of the English word "closet," or it may have come from the French word meaning enclave or vineyard enclosure.

I learned, in time, that the refined way of asking to go was to say "May I?" or "I would like to *disappear*" (*verschwinden*), but the ultra-refined way was not to disappear at all, to cut down on one's fluids and arrange to get home in time to disappear at leisure.

To add to the general misunderstanding about all things to do with plumbing, the Austrian word for a shower is the French word *douche*, while to ask to take a nice hot *douche* before dinner is met with horror in America.

86

■ ■ ■ ■ ■ ■ ■ ■ ■ ■ ■ ■ ■ ■ ■ ■ ■ ■ ■ ■

As far as the years I spent in Hoffmann's classes were concerned, I never used or ever even knew where the ladies' room or loo was. Even if I had known, I would never have wanted to create a resounding flush of thunderously gurgling water to echo and re-echo down that wide stairwell, and anyway, I was young and shy and could manage my day angelically.

CHAPTER 7

The First Days at Hoffmann's School

Mother was torn between the wish to take me to my first day of school, which she seemed to see as the opening of a finishing-school-like event, and the desire to be home for Father's birthday in early September. Much to my relief she decided in favor of Father, and I picked her up at the Bristol a few days later to see her off on the train for Paris. On the way back from the station, I bought myself a small pinkish and greasy lipstick that turned out to be slightly rancid, but it didn't matter; buying it was my first act of independence and courage. By that time I was having serious butterflies and was glad that Mother had gone so that I would be able to go to the school's opening alone, lipsticked, and most important of all, with my hair up, although paralyzed with fear.

In the early 1920s hair was the only accurate way by which age could be calculated. Girls had long hair worn down their backs and secured by hair ribbons until they were about ten. From ten to twelve the hair stayed untied, but the ribbons gave way to hoops, slides or rubber bands. Hair was barretted any old way during the awkward years until girls became *Backfische* (baked fishes) in Vienna, or Sweet

Sixteen in New York, when their hair was gathered back into a doubled-up *Mozart Zopf*, a braid, and tied with a flat black bow at the nape of the neck. This *Der Rosenkavalier* look was most becoming. When the impatiently awaited cataclysmic eighteenth birthday finally came, hair went up and nothing was ever quite the same again.

I was fourteen and wanted to look eighteen without actually pinning a knot on my head. Fortunately, it was the style in New York to twist flapperish scarves around one's head, in colors that were thought to enhance the eyes, which gave me a chance, after Mother was safely back in New York, to tuck my hair up under such a scarf and hope I looked eighteen. The uneven hemlines and indeterminate dress lengths of the day would help me to get by with certain subterfuges I had in mind. It was not done in order to deceive the school about my age—I was not even aware until recently that there had been a minimum age limit and that I had been four years under it—but rather to give myself confidence mixed with youth's eternal determination to look older than it is.

State-subsidized schools in postwar Austria did not send out brochures or publish catalogues. It is hard to believe now that I knew neither what I would be taught nor just how I would learn it. What Hoffmann gave his pupils depended entirely on that pupil's abilities and not on a set schedule. Even if I had known how Oskar Strnad, Anton Hanak and Professor Alfred Roller conducted their classes, it would not have told me what to expect from behind the closed doors marked HOFFMANN SCHULE. It was ostensibly an architectural school, but would-be dress and textile designers disappeared behind its doors, and what they were when they came out could not, as I learned later, be predicted. I know now that Hoffmann's school was planless, that he worked instinctively, impulsively and without program. I was there, and I presume my classmates were there for the same reason, because I was carried away with what I had seen of Hoffmann's work. He, in turn, accepted us because he saw some sort of qualification that he could develop.

On what I had been told would be the opening morning of school, I timed myself to be there by nine. I walked through the Stadtpark, feeling much younger than I was trying to look, to the drab building on the Stubenring that housed the Kunstgewerbeschule. There was no gathering of students at the inconspicuous door, nothing at all to suggest it was opening day. The door opened into a glassed-over atrium with wide, shallow stairs that wound up two stories. A born grumpy porter in the *Portier Loge*, who never cheered up while I was at school, directed me up to the top, where I turned left to the tall doors at the end of the corridor marked HOFFMANN SCHULE, a school within a school and my goal.

No one in Austria has ever settled whether one knocks on a door or walks in. My knocks were not answered, and I finally walked in to find school assembled and working as though it had been there forever. Not a trace of first-day

■ Oswald Haerdtl, with the omnipresent cigarette
dangling from his fingers

pleasantry, not a sound. I just stood, petrified, until some-
body finally said, *"Grüss Gott,"* "Greet God," the peasant's
salute to everyone he passes. I too said, *"Grüss Gott,"* but
it didn't help to break the ice. After several centuries a dark
young man, who looked like a wingless and peaked Melozzo
da Forli angel, smoking a crumpled cigarette which turned
out to be a permanent fixture, came out of a door on my
right and led me back through that door into a smaller room
divided into two cubicles. He sat me down on the third chair
in front of one-third of the table space in the second cubicle
and seemed to feel that his duty was done.

There was one large window facing west, and two seem-
ingly demure young women occupied the two remaining
chairs and were working on two-thirds of the working table.
There was no attempt at getting together, no introductions;
we all looked straight ahead and didn't even smile. After
an event as decisive as that first day of school, one does not
remember how one expected it to be, except *different*. But
it was not as bad as it might have been; at least Hoffmann
was not there, and the young man, who turned out to be
almost as new as I was, was Hoffmann's assistant and class
monitor, Oswald Haerdtl. He later married Carmela Prati,
the girl who was sitting right next to me, although neither
of them suspected this would happen at the time.

He had said to sit down, so there I sat, not knowing what
to do, in an agony and swallowing hard, until afternoon
when he came back to send me out to buy art supplies. The
nearby shop had little to choose from—rainbows of pastel

colors that did not look like the Hoffmann school, modeling clay and oil colors. I selected a carpenter's pencil; a box of *Kleinchen Farben*, Little Colors; an aluminum box, smaller than the palm of my hand, with ten tiny pellets of aniline colors in ten little hollows. They contained enough transparency and intensity to blind. It was not an inspiring purchase, but I didn't know what I was going to need it for.

As far as the paper was concerned, there was no choice. Whether we were beginners or famous artists, or packers and shippers, or grocers, we were all forced to use the same dirty-creamish-colored, nameless paper that was the only one available in Vienna at the time. One of the sides was glossy, the other side was dull and it came in large sheets that were folded into quarters. It was the same *Packpapier*, packing paper, that collectors now handle with reverence and pay fortunes for when the glossy side of a one-quarter sheet is covered with a faint drawing by Klimt or Schiele. For all other paper purposes, old newspapers had to do.

Everyone in class seemed to be an Old Hoffmann boy or girl, or they had come from some other teacher within the school and knew what they were doing. They were all bowed industriously over their packing paper and interrupted their work only for various food breaks. *Wurst* or *Käse Brote*, sausage or cheese on thick slabs of black bread, came out of rucksacks and back pockets and were munched at their places; there was little moving about and no conversation. The few art classes I had attended up to then had all been clustered around some sort of central object, a plaster cast or an arrangement of three green apples and a bottle, or two red apples in a basket, and we were told exactly what we were to do about it. In Hoffmann's class there was nothing to indicate what we were supposed to do. There was no model stand, no model and no teacher, and the dark young man had disappeared for good.

I sat in my third of the second cubicle with a blank mind. What little comfort I felt was in the fact that Mother had not brought me there. While the students undoubtedly had parents, none of them showed, that day or ever. I kept thinking of the story that the publisher Gordon Carroll told long ago about a man who took possession of his new yacht, in his new yachting clothes, and, with the entire crew lined up at attention said, "Well . . . . commence yachting." I said to myself, "Well . . . . commence designing," and felt just as blank and idealess as when the children in school used to ask me to say something in German, and stood around waiting expectantly while I couldn't think of anything in any language.

After a few agonizing days of just sitting there and staring at my packing paper, I finally worked myself up to a hideous little fashion sketch of a woman in a gold-and-black-plaid coat. I practically wove it, with scarf and coat blowing, standing against a steamship rail under a blue sky before a blue sea of symmetrical whitecaps. It was a popular subject

A Wimmer class at the Wiener Werkstätte ■

for New York Harbor, but out of place in the center of Europe. I followed it with various equally unpromising fashion sketches and began to breathe more normally. Several quiet days with each of us doing our own thing had lulled me into thinking that there would be time in which such atrocities could be improved and adapted to the taste I saw around me. I had almost accepted the silence and the condensed *"S'Gott"* with which we greeted each other in the mornings—even the butterflies had subsided—when, with an electrifying shock and without warning or sound, Hoffmann walked in.

He did not even remotely look like my illusory Hoffmann, not even like a proper Austrian professor; nor did he look as though he could possibly have designed all those heavenly villas and fabrics and glasses I had mooned over. At that moment I could hardly remember the Hoffmann I had dreamed up for myself, except that he was outgoing and glad to see me, that we were going to have long conversations and that he was supposed to be the original father-professor-confessor figure—charming, wise, *gemütlich*, empathetic, sympathetic, and a divine waltzer. There never was a more harmonious professor-pupil relationship than ours, as I had imagined it, but the real Hoffmann wiped it all out in an instant.

He was a very old man, at least fifty, and silent. Haerdtl said, *"Das ist die Amerikanerin"* ("This is the American"), which only deepened the silence. Hoffmann was apparently as disappointed in me as I was in him. He was a large man

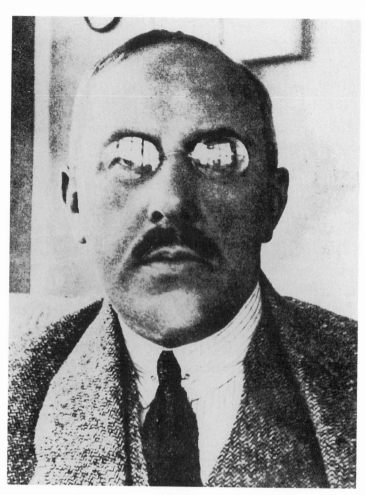

Josef Hoffmann in his characteristic pepper-and-salt tweeds, the windows of his School reflected in the lenses of his *Pinz-nez*

and although I only heard him raise his voice once above his murmured asides to Haerdtl, he looked as though he could bellow, and we looked as though we would rather not get him started. He glanced at my dreadful little drawings and walked on. I was told, long afterward, that if he had reached over my shoulder and turned them face down on the table, it would have meant complete disapproval. Leaving them face up was a good sign.

I hadn't been greeted; I didn't know a good sign when I saw one, and I didn't know that it could have been worse. It was a disappointment, a total deflation and nothing that I could escape from. Now I would call it a challenge; then it was indigestion, from which there was no turning back. I was in Hoffmann's School in Vienna, and while it was not the bed of roses I had dreamed up, it was what I had wanted, and I would never have confessed to anyone that it wasn't the fulfillment of all my dreams. I had been one of those unresponsive children who when asked each day "How was school?" had unfailingly and exasperatingly said, "Fine." When the Gerickes asked how Hoffmann had been and when I wrote home, I reported that he was "fine."

Instead of a dark frock coat or, for all I knew, a black velvet tam-o'-shanter and a blue smock, Hoffmann was a mountain of pepper-and-salt homespun and high starched collar that first time he came to class, and the last time I saw him, some years later, he was still all pepper and salt and laundered stiffness. What he said to me, in the third-person singular, during the years between, could be counted on one's fingers, and what I said to him was nothing at all. Now that I look back on all of it, it really was the most harmonious of professor-pupil relationships, unmarred by words.

While Hoffmann was setting the pace for progress in design for the world, he maintained a slightly turn-of-the-century-Scottish-moor look for himself, the blending of a man after a grouse set in a period when fashion's first demand seemed to be discomfort. He looked like a man who should be escorting a woman with a *Wespentaille*, a wasp waist, to go with his slightly abbreviated *Vatermörder*, father murderer, a particularly torturous high stiff collar. His suit looked as though it could have stood by itself, as unyielding as armor, whenever he was not in it. That first look at him in his patricidal collar was enough; gone were the pleasant conversations, the *Sympathetisch*-ness and the *Gemütlichkeit* forever.

My only comfort was that the entire class seemed to feel as I did, frightened of him, but apparently not all the time. Some years later I saw a picture of my rarely photographed Herr Professor, sitting in a painted flying machine against a painted sky beside one of my perfidious cubicle mates and one from the cubicle next door. It was one of those photographer's backgrounds through which one pokes one's head (Hoffmann's had a straw boater, or *canotier*, sitting perfectly straight on his) at fun fairs and grins into the camera. Hoffmann and his pupil-passengers were as stern

Professor Hoffmann with three pupils. Although the setting is lighthearted, the mood appears somber. Will the plane run out of fuel?

as always; one would have said, from their expressions, that they were thousands of feet up and out of fuel.

I knew from my magazines that Hoffmann had discarded, or possibly had never begun, with color; he used his black and white in a way that convinced one that color was not necessary. The white was neither warm nor cold; it was pure white. Beautifully enameled or lacquered walls or furniture were picked out with black moldings in absolute proportion and compatibility. When Hoffmann did use color, to accent

his architectural work, he did so with murals or paintings by Klimt. He was the first modern to use the shadows that forms cast, as the Persians had done, to create a design and give depth to his plain white.

Hoffmann's black and white was not a mannerism or a pretension. It was not a trademark that he affected to distinguish his work; it was the way he saw color and the way he felt about it. Black and white were his two colors; they were all he needed, and everything else only served to accentuate them. If he needed color, he used those vibrant panels by Gustav Klimt, and who would ever want more than that? I was prepared for that—it was what I wanted to see and learn—but I did not expect that he, Hoffmann himself, would be all black and white too. It was not that he wore a black suit and black fedora, or a discreet pinstripe; he came to school in a three-piece mountain of pepper-and-salt homespun; his shoes and knitted tie were black, his linen and high stiff collars were white, and all of it matched his pepper-and-salt hair and his dark clipped moustache. It was not a gracious Habsburg affair with a slightly melancholy droop at the corners, but rather an uncompromising sort of moustache that could have adorned a *Politbüro* upper lip.

I had not seen a picture of Hoffmann before I saw him in the flesh that day, but in recent years a few earlier pictures have been unearthed, and I have now seen him in knickerbockers and in black suits, even in what looks like an Austrian Prince Albert, which was called a *Gerock* or *langer Sakko*. With it he apparently always wore a slightly too small *Zylinder*—we call them top hats—on his head. The pictures were all taken at the presentations of prizes and other functions, and none of this finery showed up at school. Hoffmann had by then been in England and become a homespun man, possibly owing to his great admiration for Charles Rennie Mackintosh.

How Hoffmann looked on the street, what sort of overcoat and hat he wore, I had no way of knowing. We might have met him at the door or in the corridor as we came to class, but the Kunstgewerbeschule was not a school for lingering in cold passages, and Hoffmann was apparently just as anxious to avoid us as we were to avoid him. He must have arranged his schedule in such a way that he either came in before or after we did. We always scurried to our tables and rarely even met each other before we were in place. There we sat huddled over our packing paper, and there was J. Hoffmann, breathing hard. The man, about whom I had thought and toward whom I had dreamed and planned for four years, was a terrifying disappointment. He left class that first day as abruptly as he came in, without a word to any of us. Only the old boys and girls seemed to take him calmly and to know what to make of him. I was to learn gradually that while I did not understand Hoffmann or his classes that first day, or ever after, I was perfectly understood and would be brilliantly steered on my way by Hoffmann's method of teaching, which was, like everything else he did, entirely his own.

Even at that first encounter it was clear that Hoffmann was going to be impersonal, that he detached himself completely, but we learned in time that it was not indifference. He was serious about us as about all phases of his work, but since he had to steer and mold us he would have no nonsense, no waste of time, no useless talk and no unbending. We were not going to get around him.

I have now met several of his later pupils and hear that he mellowed with the years, but in our day his rigidity was unrelenting. Since there was no talk and no smiling, I don't even know whether he had teeth.

As I readjusted myself to the real Hoffmann and abandoned the dream one, I remembered that they did have one thing in common, the handicap that was not supposed to have prevented him from dancing. Hoffmann had poor vision, which might have been an impediment in his career, but it did not make him dependent on me as I had hoped it would when I was ten. If anything, it seemed to help him to hide. His extreme reticence and undemonstrativeness was clear even to us; he made himself inaccessible, and none of us would have dreamed of running after him for a last consultation in the corridor. We didn't even dare to ask him a question, and there was no way or opportunity to look him in the eye. He took refuge behind the reflections in his glasses and wore the kind that sat up as near to his eyes as possible. What he wore was called a *Zwicker*, *Klemmer* or *Pinz-nez*. The words need no translation; they sound exactly like what they are, pinchers. They were not invented but a gradual development that sat on thousands of noses after 1840, but on none as obstinately as on Hoffmann's. They made even-tempered people look like embittered misanthropes and disfigured many great men—see Mahler and Offenbach, whose *Pinz-nez* was gold-rimmed and black-ribboned and quivered divertingly above his moustache, wide whiskers, cleft chin and smile. The *Zwicker* was generally abandoned early in this century, when Hoffmann was about thirty, in favor of variety spectacles, which introduced so much owlish charm that they were often worn with plain glass instead of lenses, or pushed up on the forehead to enhance the hairline and the aura of studiousness. But not for our Professor Hoffmann—he clung to his *Zwicker* as his *Zwicker* clung to him. The lenses were rimless, riveted to an intricate device that pinched the top of his nose and his forehead into a vertical column that made him appear relentless. Some glasses enlarge the eyes, but Hoffmann's obscured; all one ever saw in them was oneself. I never knew what color eyes he had; it was my first impression of him, and since he never took his glasses off in my presence, it was also my last. I wonder now whether the inexplicable, the enigmatical Josef Hoffmann was vain, but with all the tempting black horn-rimmed glasses that came into style, he still wore his unbecoming *Zwicker*.

- Hoffmann's signature

CHAPTER 8

Hoffmann's School

After Hoffmann's first visit to the class, I spent the rest of my schooling in watching out for, preparing for and dreading his next one. The old boys and girls seemed to have developed some sort of extrasensory perception of his comings and goings, not sufficient that they would have dared put up their feet or chatter, but at least they seemed to know more or less when to expect him. I had to rely on an even deeper silence around me, on the feeling that the class had frozen like rabbits and after that the sound of his heavy breathing and grunting behind my back. The result of these silent surprise visits was that we tried always to be prepared for them, alert and bowed over our work, not a minute lost, not a whisper and no nonsense. No one got up and wandered: we were glued to our chairs. He was never confronted by an out-of-place pupil or a titter.

I have tried to think of words for what those months in Hoffmann's School lacked, and the only ones I can come up with are frivolity, humor and camaraderie. There was not a single lighter moment; no one had contact with anyone else. If they ever laughed, it was not while I was there. We were docile, teachable gray mice, and compared to our behavior in Vienna, the harmless gigglings and whisperings we produced at the convent in New York were high shenanigans. I think I was the only new pupil in the class, and when I looked around at the old ones for comfort or togetherness, they looked almost as terrified as I was. Time and familiarity did nothing to ease the fear of those visits, and I found no comfort in the fact that I had brought the whole thing on myself. I was exactly where I had been determined to be, in Professor Hoffmann's School in Vienna.

The Museum for Art and Industry in Vienna was founded by the art historian Rudolf von Eitelberger in 1864 along the lines of London's Kensington Museum. Its adjoining Kunstgewerbeschule, Arts and Crafts (or Trade) School, which Eitelberger directed, made itself so strongly felt that the combination of art with trade had become a *Bewegung*, a movement, before 1873, when it exhibited successfully at the Vienna World Exposition. The Kunstgewerbeschule offered the young architect Josef Hoffmann a professorship in 1899, before he was twenty-nine years old, which he accepted conditionally. He insisted on having a school of his own within the school building, which they accepted unconditionally. By the time I entered Hoffmann's School, it was a completely isolated unit entrenched behind its closed doors.

The small portfolio of sketches I had submitted to pave my way into school contained infinitesimal illustrations for Russian tales and Chinese legends, done in sparkling colors, sketches with carefully rendered microscopic brocades and laces. My largest illustrations were five-by-five inches, and most of the sketches had to be cut out of my school books, in which the blank pages had always been more inspiring than the printed ones.

My colors came in tiny porcelain pots, as large as my thumbnail, and the hairs of my brushes were numbered. I used a magnifying glass and had developed a home *pâte sur pâte* technique by dropping beads of glue here and there from the end of a pin and painting over them with gold when they were dry. I even learned to brush a breath of banana oil over them and then a tiny flake of gold leaf. The whole thing looked mighty like a Lenox service plate or a Christmas card. These dreadful little "jewels" were just what parents and Sister Miriam-Stevens at school delighted in; they even touched Joseph Urban—but not Hoffmann, the architect of the future, the ruthless searcher for essentials and simplifications. I have no doubt they were as the red cloth to the bull.

On his second visit to our cubicle, I was struggling over a decorative rider in full armor with plumes on a dappled horse, plunging over flowering shrubs against a windblown cloudy sky. It was all very reminiscent of Sherwood Forest and contained in a four-by-three-inch rectangle. He took one long silent look and said to Haerdtl, *"Sie soll es in Holz schneiden"* ("she should cut it in wood"). And so I had, in a sense, arrived. I had been addressed, albeit in the third person in doomlike tones, which, coming from Hoffmann and at second sight, could be counted as effusiveness.

After having the process of making a woodcut rather than a wood carving explained to me by Haerdtl, I went to Bier and Schöll and bought myself a small block of stone-hard pear wood and a V-shaped chisel. I should have added a vise, but I used my knees instead. After transferring the rider onto it, I worked for several hours without scratching the surface of the wood and finally went home to work over the weekend. Vienna was cold, so I took the wood to bed with me and when I finally succeeded in digging the chisel down into the wood, it plowed across the block, through several blankets and deep into my knee, where it left a small V-shaped scar that has remained to this day.

When that first woodcut was completed, it was of a riderless white horse flying over space against a clear sky, all of which was expressed in a few lines. It took far too much strength to chisel my way across an adamantine block of pear wood to waste it over feathery lines and unnecessary embellishments. No one in their right mind would use two lines, in such a medium, where one would do. Hoffmann was right and I learned my first lesson the hardwood way. Any other teacher would have said in the first person, "Your line is too fussy, your design is too busy—simplify it." Hoffmann took us across shortcuts and scarred knees to achieve in a few hours what might have taken years. Gone were my five-by-five-inch dimensions, my indispensable magnifying glass and my single sable-hair brushes. Needless to say, I never again added a *pâte sur une pâte*.

After cutting all sketches in wood, I graduated to cutting

them more simply in linoleum. I was beginning to feel content and settled in this new medium when Hoffmann strode into class one day and said, "She should paint it on the wall." The cubicle was too small, so I was moved into the large corner coeducational classroom where the walls were high and I was terrified, since I inclined to wooziness whenever I stood on a footstool.

My ordeal was made worse by the fact that the section of wall I was ordered to take over was one that Camilla Birke, the most brilliant pupil in the class, had been covering meticulously with packing paper for the last two weeks, expressly for herself. Hoffmann's orders were often brutal, but the worst were those that commanded *him* or *her*—and *her* was usually *me*—to take over another pupil's preparations. These could be, for example, a magnificently stretched piece of precious paper, a grounded canvas, a prepared wooden board, or sheets of packing paper mounted smoothly on the wall. No one knows how deeply the loss of an unblistered stretch of paper can affect one, but I did know that having to work on such a misappropriated surface, fourteen feet up, is worse than mounting it and losing it. In later years I would have apologized, replaced the paper, laughed and been forgiven, but back in school we were as speechless and inhibited as our professor, and nothing was ever said to smooth the hurt or my guilty conscience.

Hoffmann taught us nothing. If teaching meant the imparting of knowledge, then he was not a teacher. He conveyed nothing; there were no words, no advice, no critique. He did not comment; we had none of the dreamed-about discussions. He only judged, not the drawings on our boards, but what they revealed to him of our abilities and whether they were worth digging out. What we drew or modeled, what Hoffmann saw on our boards when he peered over our shoulders, did not, in fact, matter. It was not studied for its merits or its faults, but only as a disclosure of what we were. Hoffmann believed that what we could become lay within ourselves, that we could not learn it, he could not teach it, but he could discover it. The secret of his extraordinary gift for guidance was that he let nothing interfere. Words and smiles, little chats with his pupils could have been misleading, would have led to explanations, evasions and excuses, so he did not speak. The silences that I tried to explain away as a speech defect were wisdom. He knew that art could not be taught by one to another and felt that his obligation was only to recognize and develop talent.

Hoffmann never tried to fill a place in our lives; he did not play the father, the patriarch, the professor or confessor or even the teacher. He had no time for poses, although I sometimes wondered whether the flying appearances at school, with him always dressed the same way, could possibly have been an act, whether he was at heart the friendly Viennese who put on the stern-professor disguise when he came in the door. In all his non-pupil relationships he was kind. He did not find fault with us and he was patient. Once we were accepted, he dug deep for our talent, and no one was expelled.

One of Hoffmann's kindest reactions to our work was to return with a carefully dust-covered book out of his own library and put it down before the pupil whose work he had found wanting. The book was bookmarked to show the pages that should be studied, and it was picked up at his next visit, all without a word. My work was never turned over, nor was I lent a book; but Carmela Prati, who sat next to me, was brought a delightful book of Chinese toys, in which she found exactly what she needed. Other books he brought were of Chinese prints or pictures of primitive toys, but always books that he apparently treasured.

I knew from my parents that an Austrian education was a strict one, that schools started earlier and closed later and that Saturdays were school days. Vacations were measured in weeks instead of months and raps across the knuckles were not unknown. What I did not know was that an Applied Art School would be no exception. From the irascible porter through to the frowning faculty there appeared to be bad dispositions and ill humor on all sides. I think there were lighter moments and some conversation in other classrooms, but the Hoffmann *Schule* ground on along the disciplinary lines of a Prussian army camp.

The austerity of the atmosphere was not enough, however, to discourage any of Hoffmann's pupils: none of us were going to leave him because he frowned. We all knew that our Herr Professor was the best and that we could not go on to anyone else. The perfection that Hoffmann strove for in everything he did was what we wanted to learn, whether it was in fashion or architecture, textile design or interior decoration; we wanted to learn his simplifications, his beautiful detailing, his use of color and lack of it, his ingenuity and, above all, his versatility. The fact that he had accepted us constituted such an honor that to switch to another teacher in the school would have been unthinkable; even to express dissatisfaction in any way would have been a sort of treason, and to be a "drop-out" in Vienna in the early twenties was preposterous. Education in postwar Austria was far too precious in time and expenditure to be wasted; there was not one of us who was there to mark time until something better came along.

We were too close to the Hoffmann School, sitting right there in it, to see it clearly or to appreciate what was happening to us. At the time it seemed as though we were no sooner settled into a new medium and a new dimension than he tore us out of it and spun us into something else. Each of those steps was a step forward, but at the time it felt like sitting on a merry-go-round. In spite of all the spinning about, we learned the essentials: concentration, absolute dedication and appreciation. We were disciplined Hoffmann disciples for keeps.

I don't think I learned much from my fellow students, who are supposed to be, in some cases, one's greatest inspiration at school. For one thing, we were all doing something different and the other students too were being led through a turmoil of new experiences. I never saw any of them outside of school. We had no contact; the only things we had in common were Hoffmann and being cold together. I remember being touched when one of them offered me a swig of his *Achtel*, eighth, of rum on the coldest day of the year. We were serious and ill-assorted, and found it hard to communicate. They were older and spoke *Wienerisch* or *Hernalserisch*, local accents that I did not understand. They came to school on bicycles or on the minimum-fare back platforms of the tramways and they too were shy.

I remember that my parents believed that we had to go to good schools because of the friendships we would make with the right sort of people, the desirable connections that would arise from the parents and homes of our classmates. I made no connections at the Hoffmann School while I was there; we knew nothing about each other or where we were going. We were not held together after school by reports from class secretaries, by school periodicals or later by decennial reunions. I knew them too slightly to stay in touch, and they were connected to each other only by a weakening grapevine. But apparently it is not the yearly Christmas card or those depressingly mimeographed annual reports of activities, babies and deaths which cement school friendships. With the exception of a postal card from Karl Molnar, a gawky architectural student, there were no contacts or connections with my classmates. When I came back to Vienna many years later, I looked up Mela Prati Haerdtl and found

My schoolmate Carmela Prati,
who married Oswald Haerdtl

that we were friends and that we liked each other. We had grown up; we were not frightened or shy or cold, and we had all the benefits of a classmate foundation without the burdening years of unshared interests. We could talk about Hoffmann and even laugh a little.

None of us were classroom talents that faded out when we were on our own; we were a group of young designers who had been shaped into our careers, and we had been taught to be versatile, to shift within our abilities as the need arose. Hoffmann foresaw the changes that lay ahead in the fields of industrial design and quantity production, and, while he tried to stem the trend with his work in the Wiener Werkstätte, he taught us to *design,* whether it was fashion, fabrics, glass- or silverware, ceramics or furniture, costumes or jewelry, interiors or murals, postal cards or a beaded bag.

We had none of the teeming corridor life that one now finds in school buildings. There were no coffee urns; we did not troop out together to powder our noses, smoke or gossip. We only went to our classrooms and worked. Most of us brought and ate our own luncheons, worked again and went home. I can remember that I hung about in the corridor only on the one day that the Board of Judges passed on our work at the end of the first semester. The Board included the redoubtable Professor Roller, next to whom our Hoffmann was a woolly lamb. Roller was a stage designer, a late-coming Secessionist, the *Vorsitzender* ("front sitter," or head) of the school. He was morose, endlessly long and narrow, and in those clean-shaven years after beards, whiskers and sideburns had gone out of style and before the beard made its comeback, Roller was one of the few Viennese who flaunted a longish gray one. He was black-frock-coated, bespectacled and horrifying.

We all waited in agony. I remember sitting on the cold third-floor balustrade for hours, composing letters to my father to tell him I had *durchgefallen*—fallen through, or failed. Finally, an architecture student called Franz Molnár, who had his connections, brought early and still unofficial word that I had passed. We shook hands, and later that summer he sent me a postal card with greetings from a place called Ybbs. It was one of those funny Austrian names that I could not forget, and now I live near Ybbs and the Ybbs River in the Ybbs Valley.

There was nothing among my fellow pupils that hinted, even remotely, at artiness or bohemianism. They looked like the children of working people, peasants, suburban shopkeepers. Their talents and abilities justified their years at school and their family's sacrifices, and they did nothing to stamp themselves as budding artists. The only exceptions were the *Ausländer*, or foreigners—a man called Friedl from Prague; Jo Mielziner from New York, who was studying stage design with Strnad; and me, Hoffmann's *Amerikanerin*. Friedl was about to become an interior decorator. He powdered his face over with some aftershave concoction that always turned him faintly lavender. He also wore a black Fedora hat at a jaunty angle, and creamy spats. I ran into him, years later, in Prague and was dragged off to see his latest job. It was an apartment on the Wenzelsplatz, where floors were bare and maroon carpeting covered the walls. It looked as though the years with Hoffmann had not left their mark. Jo Mielziner dressed inconspicuously, carried a walking stick and overcame all his language problems by smiling. I have since asked one of my cubicle mates what I was like, and all she could remember was that I was thinner than any of them, which they attributed to tuberculosis, and that I had a peculiar walk. Actually, I slunk about in what was the approved flapper roll of the day—half camel walk and half lizard crawl. It seems I was classified as Hoffmann's AmericanGuestStudent, all one word, and was suspect because he picked me out of an all-girl cubicle and put me into the all-architectural corner room where Camilla and I were the only coeds. Furthermore, I was younger than any of them, and I now hear that I was the most "ladylike," wore pleated skirts and walked up and down stairs elegantly; I did not go up two at a time and come down four at a time.

The girl whose paper-covered wall Hoffmann made me use, Camilla Birke, was about seventeen, enormously talented and temperamental. She was the daughter of a corset-maker who rose to corset the Queen of Prussia. Camilla had a mop of frizzy hair and a deep voice and showed no signs of her better situation. She was the *star* in our class, and Hoffmann took her, Hilda Polsterer, and my second cubicle mate, Christa Erlich, along to the International Arts and Crafts Exhibition (Arts Déco) in Paris in 1925. There they helped embellish the showcases in his exhibit and promptly defected. Polsterer went over to work for Le Printemps, Camilla opened a successful fabric-design studio in Berlin and Christa Erlich became the designer for a Dutch silver firm and disappeared into The Hague. I recently heard that her former classmates, who seem to have been more human than I realized, voted her the ripest and most worldly in the class, and even considered her capable of marrying her boss. They associated her with velvet, monkey fur and fringe.

The girls from the first cubicle, Trude Höchmann and Friedl Steininger, opened a fashion salon in Vienna, from which Steininger went on to become Jaeger's designer in London. She later married our classmate Walter Loos, no relation to Adolf, with whom she opened an atelier in Buenos Aires. Eduard Wimmer, who had been a Hoffmann pupil before us, became professor and head of the Wiener Werkstätte's fashion department. Carmela Prati went to work for Caramba in Milan, where she did costume designs for La Scala and later designed fabrics in Italy until she married Haerdtl in 1927. Another earlier pupil was the renowned ceramist Wally Wieselthier, who went to America (as did Hoffmann's son Wolfgang), where he concentrated on furniture design. His first wife, Pola Weinbach, also in our class, was for many years designer for Botany Woolen Mills.

I cannot remember any evidence of romance in Hoffmann's School, but I have since discovered two cases of which I was unaware at the time. Wolfgang—Josef Hoffmann's grown son, who appeared fully armed at school one day, when none of Hoffmann's confreres knew he had ever

■ Oswald Haerdtl, apparently interrupted
while writing—or drawing?

had a child, and some did not even know he had a wife—shared his father's reticence. To begin with, he entered Strnad's class at school and did not advance to his father's class until he did so with Strnad's star pupil Oswald Haerdtl, with whom he shared a noisy motorcycle, for which he was always dressed and begoggled and beclipped.

It was the motorcycle, an asset beyond compare, which apparently caught the eye of Pola Weinbach, the pretty Polish girl in the next cubicle. She was honey-sweet, which the Viennese unfailingly explained as "Polishness," while everything that was messy was "Czechishness." Some years later, when I was working for Urban in New York, he asked Mother to meet Wolfgang Hoffmann at the steamer, for which Urban had sent him a ticket, a sponsorship and the promise of employment. Mother stood at the gangplank until all the passengers had cleared, telephoning me at intervals for ever more precise descriptions; "tall, dark, thin, eyeglasses and motorcycle clips" was all I could offer, but no Wolfgang.

He turned up in second class, where two could travel as cheaply as one, with Pola on his arm, his new and unannounced bride. The elder Hoffmann had not known of either the marriage or the departure, and Urban, who had not bargained for two Hoffmanns, canceled the employment. Urban may have been impulsive in such matters; he married Mary Porter Beegle before she could speak German or he could speak English, but he drew the line. Wolfgang went into designing furniture, Pola opened a lamp and lampshade shop in New York and, after separating from Wolf-gang, married the author Rex Stout and designed fabrics for Botany. Mr. Stout loyally placed Nero Wolfe, or maybe it was Archie Goodwin, in Wolfgang Hoffmann chairs in all his earlier books.

I met evidence of more romance when I saw Oswald Haerdtl walking hand in hand on the Ringstrasse with Mela Prati one day. Such contacts were rare in Vienna, where all intimacies like hand-holdings and parcel-carryings were forbidden. Mela Prati subsequently left to work in Italy and forgot Haerdtl, but he seems to have kept his eye on her. She attributes their marriage to her love for macaroonlike cakes that she was lingering over in a Milan tearoom, where he found her by chance just before she was to have left for good.

With the exception of Carmela Prati and Camilla Birke, talent in Austria seemed to run among the poorer classes. They knew how to work. They were there to learn, to create a future and a profession for themselves and to pull themselves out of the deprivations and the futurelessness of the war years of their childhood. They interrupted their work only to eat sausage bread. They came early and left late and no time was wasted in chattering or moving about. There was absolute concentration. I have since searched out some of the pupils and found that they followed the careers that Hoffmann started them on. A reunion in America is apt to produce large numbers of girls who "got married and had children," for whom art school was a stopgap. Hoffmann pupils may have gotten married and had children, as I did, but we all made careers in design and architecture. Hoffmann gave us a push that started us off with an impetus that could not be stopped.

I have often thought, since then, that we study at a time of our lives when we are not old or wise enough for it—that studying with as great a man as Hoffmann while we are in our teens is wasting an experience that could be infinitely more valuable at a later time. There we sat, somewhere between fourteen and twenty years old, frightened and inarticulate, being taught by J. Hoffmann and counting the minutes until he would leave the classroom.

CHAPTER 9

Hoffmann's Day

The two untranslatable German words that characterize every Austrian and his curious ways are *Gemütlichkeit* and *Schlamperei*, and the typical Viennese is both *Gemütlich* and *Schlampig*. They did not, however, hold true for Hoffmann. He lacked the carefreeness and the congeniality to be *Gemütlich* and the aimless, if charming, sloppiness to be *Schlampig*. He was at heart a sullen, almost morose and often depressed Moravian, who apparently needed and adopted Vienna for its volatileness. Hoffmann was profoundly *ungemütlich*. He did not have a shred of Urban's coziness or lovableness; he had no talent for gathering people into his warmth. No one ever snuggled down into a chair in Hoffmann's presence, to sigh with contentedness and well-being. He had only a small gift for making himself agreeable, but a fantastic talent for making his client's surroundings agreeable, for finding his way into their wishes.

As far as *Schlampigkeit* was concerned, he might be held up as its antithesis, its opposite. It means slovenly untidiness, unpunctuality and laziness all rolled together with glamour. Hoffmann was pathologically orderly, and he came from a well-regulated and orderly home that had once been the *K.u.K.* post office of Pirnitz, where his father was the mayor for a time. Young Hoffmann was slightly overweight, had poor vision, was always dignified, and only his doting sisters dared call him "Peppo." Sons of ex-mayors in the Austrian monarchy were always "intended" for something, and Josef was heading, reluctantly, for the bar when he sidestepped into the Applied Art School in Brünn and instantly blossomed. He sailed on to Hasenauer's classes in Vienna and was soon Otto Wagner's assistant at the Academy. By the time he was twenty-nine, in 1899, he was a Professor at the Kunstgewerbeschule, had a flowing black moustache, always wore hats that were one size too small for him and seems to have become set in his secretive ways.

I soon realized that I was not going to learn about Hoffmann from his pupils and least of all from him. All I knew about how he lived his day was what I saw, and that no longer coincides with recently discovered facts. I thought at the time, and have continued to think since, that Hoffmann occasionally flew through his classes at school to fulfill some compulsory professorial obligation for which he had little time. I naturally assumed—since we never encountered him in the school corridors or on the stairs, since he was always out of breath when he arrived in class, not as breathless as Wimmer but panting, and since he always wore what could only be interpreted as his street clothing, including spats—that he was indeed fresh from the street. I thought then, and took comfort in the thought, that Hoffmann probably had a design studio and an architectural office as well as a home, all of which I wishfully placed in one of the remotest outlying districts of Vienna, as at Nussdorf, where he was safely out of our way. None of us knew and did not dare to ask whether he still had a wife.

As far as his transportation to and from school was concerned, I made myself no pictures. Hoffmann was certainly not one to ride on tramways or streetcar platforms, and in those days only frowned-upon war profiteers owned cars. His son Wolfgang, which was how we knew our Herr Professor had had a wife, was completely under the thumb of the ancient motorcycle that he owned jointly with Haerdtl and which he wheeled lovingly into the school building rather than expose it to the elements. Wolfgang Hoffmann affected goggles, pushed up over his hairline, and trousers that were furled into bicycle clips at his ankles. Haerdtl did not dress the part of a half-motorcycle-owner, but had to pay his share reluctantly when his co-owner wrecked it. Young Hoffmann's offers of "Spins," seated on the saddle behind him, were generous, but such pillionage was far too hazardous and unconventional, and did not suit his father at all. Our Herr Professor had to maintain his dignity and his immaculate white-in-summer and gray-in-winter spats. Everyone had to go everywhere on foot, but having inventively established Hoffmann in outer Nussdorf, far beyond walking distance, I was forced to think of his transport in terms of one of Vienna's decrepit, extravagant and rare taxicabs, the rarer the better.

I am recounting my recollections mixed with what seem to have been my fancies about Hoffmann's day at this time before I am forced to alter them by the actualities I am now having to face. I find, with retroactive dismay, that there was no suburban atelier/office, no villa in Nussdorf and no distance between us. Hoffmann never lived in a Hoffmann house but in Vienna in the fourth *Bezirk*, about six blocks from where I lived with the Gerickes. According to Viennese standards, he was practically a neighbor. Even worse is the recent discovery that while I was thinking of him in that costly taxicab, rushing into the school building, running up those two flights of shallow steps, shedding hat, gloves and overcoat on the way, meeting Haerdtl at some appointed spot before advancing on the class in quick-step and tandem formation, he was right *there* all the time in the room next to ours, only one thin wall away.

I now know the sort of things I was not apt to know at the time, that part of Hoffmann's deal with the Austrian state was that his school would be within the Kunstgewerbeschule and that his own architectural office and design atelier, his drafting room and his private, dark, secluded and top-secret *Bureau* would adjoin it. His pupils had the light three-windowed corner room with its two cubicles beyond which was a rarely used door into a room that had a separate entrance from the corridor. This door opened in so that one could not see the room into which Haerdtl, Wolfgang Hoffmann and an all-male group disappeared and had the courage to make rather more noise than we did. They were actually heard to talk. I thought they went to smoke those appalling home-rolled, leaves-from-the-floor-of-the-Vienna-Woods cigarettes that Haerdtl constantly held in his cupped hand. We never saw beyond that connecting door into what turns out to have been Hoffmann's drafting room, and it seems that those privileged designers and draftsmen and Tusnelda von Zülow, the blonde secretary who always used the corridor door, never saw beyond the following door, which led into a small entry and from there into Hoffmann's inner secrecy. One speaks of the people who never let their left hand know what the right one is doing, but Hoffmann never let either hand know what he was doing.

Hoffmann's day at school, the reconstructed one, began with his change of appearance, when the honorable professor in street wear gave way to the hardworking designer. The alteration was effected in the space between the double doors that opened from the corridor into his drafting room. This desirable space, which corresponded with the thickness of the carrying walls, has been lost to the world but can still be found in pre–two world wars hotels, palaces, elderly apartment houses and public buildings along the Ring. Where such doors still exist, they serve to insulate against cold and sound; they also make lovely hiding places for children and in the old hotels they are the places where one finds one's brushed clothes and polished shoes in the morning. (Today actually what one finds is a shoe-polishing machine near the elevator.) Hoffmann paused in this space, in which a mirror, shelf and hooks had been installed, to hang up his overcoat and jacket, to take off his *gilet*, waistcoat and collar, and remove his beautifully starched and cuff-linked wide white cuffs. He hitched up his sleeves and braces, donned his black work coat and stepped into the little entry with his drafting room on the left and his sanctum, his retreat, opposite. I wondered then and still wonder how he determined the exact moment at which to stop his own work and visit his school, whether he was at the end of an assignment or whether his foot had fallen asleep. Possibly it was a pang of conscience that stirred him when his professorial stipend reached him or the need to stretch, or maybe just the sudden urge to get it over with. I do know from sitting at the receiving end of his visits—and I think it all rather endearing—that he re-dressed for the purpose. He got back between the double corridor doors and shed his black work coat, put on his *gilet* and jacket and adjusted his cuffs. With Haerdtl, also in jacket with cigarette, he took the six steps into the *Schule* that sent our twenty or so hearts into our twenty or so mouths. After the shortest possible visit, they left as they had come and played the whole thing back in reverse. Six paces to their door, the careful removal of cuffs, the return to his cotton coat and the retirement to his office and work, closing his door firmly behind him. He may have changed his teaching style later, but in those days we might not have seen him again for several weeks.

Long before Hoffmann arrived at school, his office factotum, Herr Diemer—who was with him for many years and knew all the ins and outs of Herr Professor's requirements, as well as those ins and outs of Hoffmann's little related foibles and fringe activities—prepared for the day. He sharpened three number-one soft black pencils with a penknife by hand, and placed them meticulously where they were wanted on the work table. After all, no one wanted an idea to be lost for lack of a pencil. Office history insists that there were always only three pencils, which I think meant that Hoffmann liked to wear them down to stubs before he embarked on three fresh ones. The relationship between a designer and his pencils is a very intimate one; I remember that Joseph Urban could not function unless he had twenty-four Boston Pencil Sharpener–pointed pencils, including reds and blues at his right hand, and even I need my twelve Faber-Castell number 2001s before I can think.

After that, the factotum folded the eternal graph-paper sheets, on which Hoffmann always worked, into quarters and cut some of them down further to fit into Hoffmann's pockets. He put out watercolors, just in case, and hung out the black cotton work coat, cut along orphanage lines, that Hoffmann always wore to distinguish himself from his draftsmen, who wore the conventional white work coats. There was no time when Hoffmann forgot his personal dignity. Everything was put in its proper place, tidy, accustomed and to hand. The blonde Tusnelda, also of many years' standing and still blonde, arrived later and sat at a table in the drafting room. There were never more than three draftsmen at one time.

Hoffmann was an all-out orderly man; a passionate orderliness underlay the basis of his design, and he did his work as neatly and systematically as he did everything else. He lived and dressed and always combed his hair with absolute precision. Now that some of his former pupils have reached an age of unwisdom and indiscreetness, and now that one or two of them are, so to speak, letting down what is left of their own hair, I was told that our Herr Professor was a bore on the subject of order. He had been born into an age of artistic clutter combined with a heavy leaning backward onto several classical periods at the same time. If a new direction blossomed, it was on the florid side and only tended to increase the confusion. Hoffmann abhorred all the mixed-up muddle; and his first reaction was to straighten out the curves. The *Jugendstil* presented him with nothing but curves, for which he substituted uniformity, harmony and straight lines. It was the simplification and the fittingness that later constituted the fine difference between his *Secession* and the *Jugendstil*.

Hoffmann's design was not impulsive. He was not one to fall out of bed in the middle of the night to put down an idea; nor did he draw on matchbox covers or on tablecloths. He worked at his properly arranged work table, or he sketched on the cut-to-size graph paper in his pocket. No backs of

■ Hoffmann's sketches for crystal, showing
one of Hoffmann's characteristic monograms

- A Hoffmann drawing of a chandelier

envelopes for him, no crumpled creations were ever forgotten in a back trouser pocket. The simple precision of his work was only possible when it was done simply and precisely, to which he added his almost pathological reticence and his ability—we should say "talent"—to hold his tongue. Words were never substituted for drawings; nothing that he did was replaced by or depended on a verbal explanation. He had nothing to say, only to draw.

When he started to work, there was never a search on the paper; there was no putting down of light feathery lines in order to find the right one among them. The entire meaning of making a sketch, a draft, did not exist for Hoffmann. He simply put down his soft black pencil on his prepared graph paper and drew a finished drawing, without hesitation, as simply as though he were writing instead of drawing. The verb "to doodle" is defined as to draw or scribble idly; it implies aimlessness. But what Hoffmann had was perfect aim and purpose. He was able to draw with complete concentration and engrossment, yet he had the ability to put it down as simply as if he were doodling it.

The Viennese invariably strove for refinement—the wearing of gloves, the bowing, the heel-clicking and hand-kissing. Their children wore white pinafores, and they injected a French word wherever possible into their conversations. But they were given to speaking less elegantly and at moments expressed themselves as their washerwomen might. So it was that I heard from an irreproachable ladylike lady this telling description of how Hoffmann sketched: "like a frog laying eggs," a process that few of us have witnessed. However, although Hoffmann did turn out his sketches in lightning succession, finished, flawless and final, hatching them was left to Haerdtl. Hoffmann drew involuntarily, spontaneously, and he released his drawings as they fell from his hand. He did not follow through, but immediately went on to the next, a continuation of the first but not a repetition. He never developed a drawing or corrected it; he never drew beyond that first soft-black-pencil sketch, which Oswald Haerdtl later interpreted for one of the current draftsmen. But Hoffmann did not let go of a project when he let the sketch go. As far as I know, there are no designers, and have never been any, whose work left their hands as early on as Hoffmann's did, yet who still exercised such strong control over it. He was the *boss*, and in the end there was not a shadow of difference between his sketch and the finished product. It was Haerdtl's hand that carried Hoffmann's small soft-pencil sketches to the drafting board and translated them into working drawings. His was the eye that oversaw all projects, and his was the pen that kept the working journals we can still see today. If it had not been for Hoffmann's decisiveness, his ability to put everything down once and for all, and Haerdtl's ability to pick up the instant Hoffmann raised his pencil from his paper, Hoffmann would not have been able to spend the second part of his day, as it turned out, in the coffee house, or *Kaffeehaus*.

■ ■ ■ ■

- When Hoffmann drew, he simply put down his number-one soft black pencil on his specially prepared graph paper and made a finished drawing—like these.

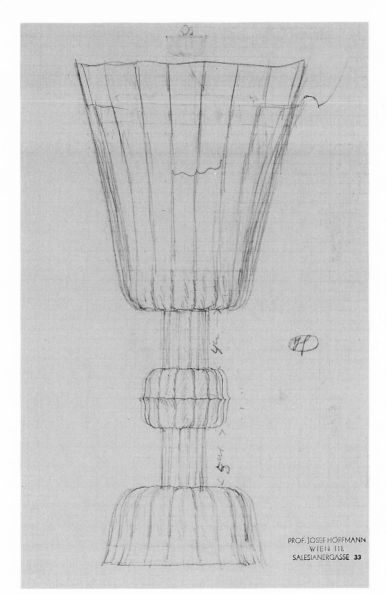

PROF. JOSEF HOFFMANN
WIEN III.
SALESIANERGASSE 33

Both the Secession, founded in 1898, and the Wiener Werkstätte, which was organized in 1902, were the result of coffee house discontent and endless inflammatory discussions—all conducted *sotto voce* in order not to disturb those patrons who came there to doze.

Long ago, Johannes Brahms always took his hour-long after-luncheon nap in the Café Heinrichshof and went there expressly for that purpose. Hoffmann did not go to the *Kaffeehaus* to sleep, but since he never permitted outsiders in school and kept his home completely secret—or possibly because he kept it completely unheated—he seems to have made the coffee house the center of his activities. It was from the Heinrichshof and the Sperl, among others, that he launched his bitter anti-*Künstlerhaus*, antiestablishment and anti–mass-production campaigns. Since the *Kaffeehaus* was Vienna's great escape hatch, the place where men became invisible, he presumably added his escape from school, office and home to the other pleasures it afforded him.

The Viennese coffee house, once called the *Kaffeehaus* and later the *Wiener Café*, was so different from the larger Parisian, Roman and Berlin cafés that the name should not confuse them. In France, Italy and Germany, cafés were often open-air or glass-enclosed, and all chairs faced the street. The object was to watch life and the passing crowd go by while eating ices and drinking coffee as well as alcoholic beverages. Saucers piled up to indicate the guests' rising indebtedness and waiters did not have the time to advise the patrons in legal, medical or marital matters; the headwaiter was not a father confessor. Men and women patronized these establishments, whereas in Vienna women were tolerated on Saturdays and Sundays, but even then they were usually shunted away into the *Damen Zimmer*, the ladies room, which meant a room with less smoke, better upholstery, hot chocolate, pastries, frivolous dogs and mirrors, rather than meaning the ladies' lavatory.

With women came music, and whereas this added to Beethoven's income and gave Lanner and Johann Strauss their openings, the true *Kaffeehaus* men stayed among themselves and drank coffee. Considering all the spoiled and pampered palates in Vienna, it is strange that the quality of the coffeehouse coffee was unimportant and often poor. What mattered was the clientele—just *who* could be seen where and *who* met *whom* there. One good literary or dramatic, artistic or political *Stammtisch* (a table at which the same members met daily or weekly and said the same things) made the café. An architectural *Stammtisch* was a feather in the owner's cap. Everyone else followed, if only to envy, defame, slander, gnash their teeth, listen in and, of course, quote.

Except for a few window seats, reserved for the same sort of elderly men who sit in their club windows in New York, the Viennese café occupants faced *in*. They read the papers, made faces, smoked, napped, transacted business and watched each other play chess or billiards. They kibitzed at tarok and dominos, gave advice and eavesdropped. Having made every effort to escape the outside world, they did not want to watch it going by. They developed café friendships and elaborate café ignorings, silences and contacts, indifferences and differences. The members of Hoffmann's *Stammtisch* had homes, bureaus, offices, ateliers (it was still the period for French words), studios, and besides that, they had stipendiary spaces in the *Akademie* and the *Kunstgewerbeschule*, and in other state-subsidized localities. But they did not use them; they preferred to practice professions, to consult their tax advisers, pick their teeth or frown on their competitors through the smoke layers in their cafés. Hoffmann was reticent and secretive; he let no one into his inner office, locked himself away when he was working on a competition, but he sat and talked, as in a goldfish bowl, in his café.

Once inside the café doors the shy were known to become bold, the loquacious were apt to turn laconic and the habitually speechless, for example our *Herr Professor*, became verbose. The decompressed Hoffmann hung his overcoat and hat on his accustomed tree, sat down among his confreres at his *Stammtisch*, signaled for his coffee and began to talk. It was all before our time, and we never saw him at it, but judging by results he could turn from being the sedate professor at school into the high-powered *provocateur* and artistic rabble-rouser all within a few city blocks. It needed a very different Hoffmann from the one we knew to inflame Gustav Klimt, Otto Wagner, Joseph Olbrich and Koloman (Kolo) Moser into concerted secession.

Hoffmann's departure for the café at noon was the end of his day at school; he never came back in the afternoon, and had I known all that, I would have breathed easier. I now hear that his draftsmen supposed that he spent the rest of the day at the Wiener Werkstätte, visiting clients and poking around all the places where he found old toys for his toy collection, but in the bottoms of their Viennese hearts, they suspected that he was sitting somewhere in a warm café.

CHAPTER 10

The Wiener Werkstätte

The founding of Hoffmann's Wiener Werkstätte, the Viennese Workshop, in June 1903 was, in a way, a continuation of the Secession of 1897. Both were the result of the dissatisfaction and discontent of an enormously creative group of young artists who had found and supported each other. In the case of the Secession, it was their defection from an established organization that did not recognize them; in 1903 it was the founding of a workshop to combat the rising wave of poor design and to create the complete work of art in the union of artist and craftsman.

Both the Secession and the Wiener Werkstätte, which we, as Hoffmann always did, will henceforth call the WW, were long before my time. When I arrived in Vienna in the early 1920s the Viennese were trying to gather themselves together after the war, and their recollections of the great artistic events of the golden prewar years had been clouded by the profound loss Vienna's art world suffered in 1918 when Otto Wagner, Gustav Klimt, his protégé the young Egon Schiele with his pregnant wife, and Kolo Moser all died and left Vienna bereft. Even I, who knew their work only from pictures, felt impoverished and could only guess at Hoffmann's personal and professional sorrow.

By the time I heard the story of the founding of the WW, it sounded as though most of it had taken place in congenial cafés while the artists relaxed on plush-covered banquettes and enjoyed hermetic sealing. There had been much talking during the early years of the twentieth century. It had been a time of artistic confusion and involution. Creative artists wrestled, partly at their easels and partly at their coffee-house tables, to gain recognition and support; but the only place where they found strength was in numbers. No one was going to, or could, go it alone. *Bunde, Klubs* and work-shops sprang up on all sides and disagreed with each other. There were *Bewegungen,* movements, and constant new *Stile,* styles; causes and trends proliferated. Whenever a few en-raged young artists gathered together at their *Stammtisch,* someone made a motion that they should form an associa-tion, and first thing they knew, there was still another *Künst-lerverband* or *Verein.* Klimt and Hoffmann had their Secession, and even student Egon Schiele led his young following out of the Academy into his new *Kunstgruppe.* They were like so many sheep following their leaders, even to the Hoffmann anti-artificial-potted-plant group that followed him out of the Café Kremser one day, never to return.

The seven founding members of the Siebener Klub, the Club of the Seven, which had been active in the Secession, went so far in their urge for togetherness that they dreamed up an artist's colony in which they were all going to live together happily ever after in beautiful Olbrich houses on land donated by the Crown. It was to be, and parts of it still are, on the *Höhe Warte*, the High Wait, in the outskirts of Vienna, looking into the *Wienerwald*, the Vienna Woods. The project had reached the planning stage when Olbrich was called to Germany, where he was appreciated and made much of, and Hoffmann took over the idealistic colony. It never did contain a Hoffmann House (his own), there or anywhere else.

Several elaborately conceived, meticulously detailed, tall and surprisingly half-timbered residences were designed by Hoffmann and constructed between 1900 and 1903. The timbers, I am told, were painted blue, and the houses were a conglomeration of Secession and Hoffmann and rural England, with touches of Pirnitz. They combined a faintly rustic look, which they call the *Volkloric-Stil* here, rolled into one with skill, luxurious dimensions and Hoffmann's orderly layouts. Among them is the Moll-Moser house, which consisted of two homes coupled together into a single plan for the painter Carl Moll and the designer-painter Koloman Moser and their families and professions, semiattachment at its best on the *Höhe Warte*.

The Hoffmann-Moser friendship dated back to their Hasenauer student days at the Vienna Academy in 1892, when Hoffmann was fresh from his studies at Brünn and his year of building army barracks in Würzburg. He was new to Vienna and the three-year-older Moser acted as his cicerone;

144

■ A WW brass cigarette box,
given by Hoffmann to the Haerdtls

in other words he showed Hoffmann around. They had gone
through the great storm and strife of seceding together; they
were both among the original seven at the Club of the Seven,
and Kolo Moser later married Ditha Mautner-Markhof, a
Hoffmann pupil, and lived in his half of Hoffmann's Moll-
Moser House. Moser, with Hoffmann and Fritz Waerndorfer, was one of the Wiener Werkstätte's founding members and was deeply involved in its *look*, which was partly
of his own creation. As time went on, Moser, the brilliant
graphic designer, took on almost all the posters, *Reklame*
(advertising), announcements and myriad printed words that

issued from the Werkstätte, even to the rubber stamp that put a beautifully lettered PAID on all receipted bills. Moser was one of the Werkstätte's most versatile designers and also its handwriting.

Hoffmann was the inspiration and the exhilaration, the endlessly creative talent; Moser was the driver and the shepherd—he spurred and he organized. He understood and sympathized with Hoffmann's search for perfection and his determination to establish the *Gesamtkunstwerk*, the total work of art. Moser was a fanner of flames, a shot in the arm, an inspired graphic designer and a good "fine artist." He also knew lots of people, had, so to speak, been around and had married well. Marrying well in Vienna meant marrying into money.

Their various recollections of how the Wiener Werkstätte was founded had become almost primitive in their simplicity by the time I heard them. It seems that in the spring of 1903, at the end of one of their customary daily *Stammtisch*, or luncheons, at the Café Kremser or the Café Heinrichshof, where Wagner, Moser, the banker Waerndorfer and a few others had been listening to Hoffmann's habitual riding of his *Steckenpferd*, his total-work-of-art hobbyhorse, and the deplorable state of art in Austria in general, someone—no one now remembers who it was—made a motion that they should form an association, with Fritz Waerndorfer, who had also married well and inherited a fortune besides, providing the money. It was not a new idea, but it came at a time when Hoffmann had just decorated Waerndorfer's apartment, beautifully, and after six years of Secession exhibitions had gradually introduced Vienna to more decorative art. On May 19, 1903, they registered *Die Wiener Werkstätte*, the Vienna Workshop, which was to shape, had they but known it then, twentieth-century design. Most of all, it shaped the enlistment of what they called "fine artists" into the field of applied art and design and they foreran into the new field of what was to become industrial design.

Having been a dream for a long time before it became a reality, the Wiener Werkstätte was ready to begin the day it was organized. They started with three craftsmen and opened their first premises in October of the same year. Hoffmann and Moser were similar artists and designers with the same integrity, the same aims and ambitions. Their talents and their abilities were the same, whether they called themselves the Club of the Seven or the Secession or, in 1903, the Wiener Werkstätte. The way it seemed to me from New York was that they were simply geometrizing, monochromizing and simplifying all the *Stile* of the end of the nineteenth century. The founding of the Wiener Werkstätte was certainly not as simple as they told it; it had been fomenting for a long time, but it was the combination of their curious talents that made everything they did possible.

Had Hoffmann been only an architect, and had Klimt been a run-of-the-mill easel painter without curiosity, had he not branched out into murals and decorations, clothes and graphic designs, and had Kolo Moser confined himself to lettering, had he not painted and illustrated, reformed women's clothing and designed books, nothing would have happened.

What made up the basic ingredients of the WW was the way in which the work of its members overlapped, their enormous versatility and the ability to draw clearly and understandably. To all of which must be added their sympathy and understanding for each other and their love for what they were doing as well as Herr Waerndorfer's willingness to invest two fortunes.

One had the feeling with all the Viennese artists—those that I later knew and saw at work, and those that I could only judge by their drawings—that they worked quickly, that they completed their work in their heads and then took up their pencils and wrote it down. Actually they might draw an elevation of a cottage, a vase, a sleeping woman, but it all seemed to come as easily as though they had indeed written down the words. They never seemed to look for their drawings on the paper; they never lifted their pencils from the paper or went over a line. It was the school of *hinschreiben*, the writing down of one's work instead of drawing it. They called it *Aus dem Ärmel schütteln*, shaking it out of the sleeves.

When Hoffmann put down one of his forms, it might be anything. One needed the customary dime to measure its scale; without the dime one never knew whether he was conceiving a bud vase or a tall column, the handle of a spoon or the long narrow windows on the Stocklet Palais's street elevation. He did not repeat himself, but he designed forms

148

- My two very large silver bowls with pedestals, designed by Hoffmann

- My Hoffmann silver coffee service

classical in their simplicity and universal in their use. If the word "all-rounder" had not come to mean a kennel club judge of all dog breeds, it would have personified Hoffmann and all the members of the WW who gradually gathered around him.

It became an organization in which Dagobert Peche designed that perfect gold-and-white wallpaper called "Water," along with delicate silver birds, mirrors, tea and coffee sets, delightful ivory and silver cigarette boxes and on top of that exquisite doilies and lace. At the same time, the graphic designer Carl Otto Czeschka was lured from his path to do remarkable silver- and metalware, jewelry and furniture, while young Oskar Kokoschka, his pupil, did illustrations and picture postal cards. During the first two years, Hoffmann and Moser did all the designing; after that, the WW developed into a series of workshops presided over by twelve able all-rounders, whose designs covered the entire field of applied art, and more than thirty-six master craftsmen who executed their designs. They were able to take over the interiors of Hoffmann's architectural assignments, and Gustav Klimt designed murals for Hoffmann's projects. Egon Schiele, Klimt, Kokoschka and all the others contributed designs and postal cards, an outgrowth of the postcard games they had played when they were young students.

The first pictures I ever saw of WW objects were in those same issues of *Deutsche Kunst und Dekoration* magazine, in which I had originally discovered my love for the flat, dec-

A Hoffmann sterling silver dinner service, made by
C. Hugo Pott

orative and largely black and white designs by J. Hoffmann.
There was an intermixture of their two names; Hoffmann's
interiors were executed by the Wiener Werkstätte, and Wiener Werkstätte objects were, in turn, designed by J. Hoffmann. It was only after I came to Vienna that I found they
were, in a sense, one and the same.

More and more artists and artisans joined the WW group,
and the work they produced was shown at expositions, exhibitions and the Wiener Werkstätte branches in Europe
and, for a short time, in New York. The most surprising

thing about the organization was the amount of work it was able to produce, the progress that it made toward the recognition of the applied arts and the fact that it worked in complete harmony. In a city that specialized in enmity, schisms, secessions and criticism, there was never talk of dissatisfactions, of disruptions or split-ups at the WW. When the WW was forced to close in 1930, it was for lack of money, not for lack of agreement within its ranks.

My professor and his cohorts' talents covered every known field of art and design, but did not extend to the art of making money. They were modest men but extravagant designers; no expense was ever spared to produce the perfect object. And whenever Hoffmann was told about costs, he expressed surprise that the end amount had four times exceeded the estimate or that the bid had been eighty percent too low or that the wolf was at the door. There were several business reorganizations and refinancings, and fortunately the fashion department went far toward keeping the Werkstätte afloat. Hoffmann advocated the use of silver in place of gold, semiprecious stones instead of diamonds, but the workmanship that went to achieve perfection ate up the economies.

Josef Hoffmann-comma-architect was the way the German lexicons defined him, which did not take into account his universality and his completeness. What he practiced cannot be defined as many-sidedness, but rather as a total unawareness of all boundaries. As long as he had his black pencil in his hand, there were no limitations to what he could design. Hoffmann was among artists what the general practitioner was to medicine, a man who understood every phase of his field and knew what was needed. His own talent was extraordinary; his ability to assemble a group of artists to work with him in the WW, who had, or learned to have, the same artistic ambidexterities was the real wonder. What he did would have been dilettantism in a less talented man, a smattering of knowledge, but Hoffmann was able to design the largest building project and the frailest long-stemmed wineglasses for Lobmeyr with equal geniality and the same black pencil. His talent lay in applying his abilities uniformly to everything he touched, not in being a gifted architect who just happened to want to relax over a little fabric design or to play with a bookplate. Hoffmann did not indulge himself; there were no amateurishnesses, no artistic hobbies, although I have since heard, darkly, that he loved to go to masked balls in homemade costumes of his own design. Everything he did was as good as everything else he did, except perhaps his deplorable gathered lamp shades. He was perfectly balanced and, as I found out years later, he expected the same from us.

The founding of the WW turned Hoffmann's many hopes and plans into a reality; he proved it possible for a group of artists to work with a group of artisans and produce the total work of art he had envisioned. Hoffmann never lectured, rarely wrote articles or broke the silences around him, but he was heard to hold forth and even wrote on the *Ge-samtkunstwerk*. The phrase actually stemmed from Richard Wagner, who was also searching for the complete work of art, but in his case one presumes that it was to be totally operatic and totally Wagnerian.

• Hoffmann on his 3-schilling stamp with a proper WW border

CHAPTER 11

The Persecution of Klimt and Schiele

My reading on the steamer from New York to Italy after graduation had been *The Divine Comedy*, largely to impress my fellow passengers. For train-travel literature through Italy to Vienna, I descended to paperbound Tauchnitz editions of the British ladies, Mrs. Bella Lowndes, Vernon Lee and Elinor Glyn (with the exception of the forbidden *Three Weeks*), and on arrival in Vienna I discovered its tempting bookshops and read everything there was to read on Klimt and Schiele. My sorrow over finding that they had died in 1918, before I got there, was further overshadowed by the shocking discovery that they had both been misjudged and badly treated, persecuted and tormented at the hands of their fellow Austrians. I read about *Die Klimt Affäre*, the Klimt incident, also called *Der Klimt Skandal*, and a heartbreaking little volume called *Egon Schiele im Gefängnis*, Egon Schiele in Prison, with horror and disappointment. I mourned for every bad minute and every disillusionment that those two had ever had to suffer.

In spite of the fact that the Austrians have always been proud of their culture, which they call *Kultur* as though it were spelled with four *o*'s, and depend upon its attractions to further their tourist trade today, they have always shown a talent for denigrating their artists and painters and for refusing to recognize them during their lifetimes. What made it worse was that the greater the artist and the more recognition and acclaim he seemed to receive from the public, the more the powers stood in his way. In the middle of the nineteenth century, the Salzburg artist Hans Makart was an exception, but so was his work. It was gigantic and Rubens-like, and even Austria and the Court could not ignore his saturated red velvets and so much flesh so voluptuously handled in so short a time. Makart died, presumably exhausted, at forty-four, after designing the procession that celebrated the Emperor Franz Joseph's and the Empress Elisabeth's Silver Wedding Anniversary. It circled the city along the new Ringstrasse and ended in the dramatically costumed and superbly mounted figure of Makart himself riding alone on a black horse and stealing the show. Vienna, the city of many *Stile*, styles, had early inaugurated the *Makart Stil*, which lasted until the *Secession Stil* took over. His enormous historical canvases had the added attraction of containing partially draped sirens and enchantresses whose faces were not unfamiliar to the Viennese public; whether their bodies were was the question. Makart had a sense of his own P.R.; after him it was difficult for any painter to make himself felt, least of all his modest follower and pupil Gustav Klimt. On Makart's early death, it was Klimt and his brother who completed Makart's then unfinished commission in the best Makart *Stil*.

I had originally faced toward Vienna full of dreams of Hoffmann, but during the years while I finished school in New York, I added the entire Secession to my idolizations, along with the memories of Klimt and his cat and his glorious paintings. When I got there, I found that writers and musicians were clasped to Vienna's heart: Arthur Schnitzler was venerated for every word he wrote; Johann Strauss was idolized; Hugo Wolf and Gustav Mahler were proudly claimed; even Johannes Brahms, who was born in Hamburg, was lauded as an adoptive son. The actors Alexander Girardi (for whom a hat was named) and Josef Kainz could do no wrong, but Gustav Klimt was insulted, ridiculed and impoverished by the Austrian government, and Egon Schiele was imprisoned and made to witness the burning of one of his sketches in a small town on the Danube for drawing women in what the town judge said were suggestive poses.

Every time I read about the unbelievable way the Academy treated Klimt, who was suggested for a professorship on four different occasions during his life, but was always refused (while it seemed to me that professorships had been handed out indiscriminately), I went back to look at his sparkling paintings and took comfort from them and the fact that he looked happy on available photographs taken in his garden with Emilie Flöge. The *Skandal* had been over Klimt's three panels depicting Philosophy, Medicine and Jurisprudence for the ceiling of the Vienna University's *Aula*. They were rejected, reaccepted and refused again, and the

■ Gustav Klimt, in 1908

payment for them had to be refunded, which impoverished Klimt. It seems the doctors of philosophy wanted to be symbolized by an old man with a long white beard opening a large tome, rather than by nudes. Jurisprudence was to have contained a blindfolded justice, draped and holding a scale, and the university's doctors wanted to be typified by an Aesculapius rather than by what they considered indecently exposed female figures that might be harmful to medical students. It seemed to me, with retroactive resentment, that they were at the university to study the healing of the human body, unclothed. And all this in a city that had lived for more than thirty years with Makart's seductresses in bits of chiffon.

Egon Schiele fared no better at the hands of small-town Austrianism. Klimt, the born Viennese, suffered under the unbelievable animosity of his Viennese adversaries. Schiele, who was born in Tulln, pronounced "tooln," a small town on the Danube in Lower Austria, suffered at the hands of villagers in the very landscape he loved so much and painted so beautifully. They were both men who should not have had to lose time over the freakish moralities and whims of their fellow artists and fellow Austrians. They both aroused fanatical hostilities for no other reason than their talent.

Children usually outgrow their first infatuations and advance from wanting to be circus riders to more serious objectives, but I cannot remember ever wanting to do anything other than return to Vienna to study design. I dreamed my dream and made it happen, not realizing that part of my goal was lost before I reached it. With the exception of Hoffmann, all my stars had died. But I did have thirty-five dollars a month allowance, and that bought me a drawing or a book each month, even a copy of Schiele's *Im Gefängnis*, which was published in 1922. All except the little Schiele book was lost when our house burned to the ground in 1973, but I lived my life, in New York and in Connecticut, surrounded by the drawings and watercolors of the two men I had appreciated at a time when a month of doing without milk-chocolate bars had bought me a piece of their work.

Just recently there was an exhibition at the Art Academy, from which Schiele finally resigned. It was entitled "*Egon Schiele vom Schüler zum Meister,*" Egon Schiele from Pupil to Master, and consisted of drawings and watercolors from 1916 to 1918. The thousands of visitors who attended were left with the strong impression that Schiele had been the Academy's favorite son, but in the thousands of fifteen-dollar catalogues that were sold, Serge Sabarsky's introduction is more truthful, although the frontispiece is a *Profil Mort* of the Academy.

The exhibition contained 105 drawings and watercolors, and was so crowded that six-deep columns of people could only pass very slowly through the two exhibition halls. Vienna appreciates its artists, sixty-six years later, with crowds that reminded me of pictures seen long ago of Rudolph Valentino's funeral.

I went back to Vienna with memories of the 1914 bicycle rider and Mother's parasol, of Klimt in his smock and the shimmer of gold on the walls around him. I was prepared for Klimt as part of the Vienna I longed for, but Schiele was just a name. My first encounter was a narrow life-sized black-crayon drawing of an extraordinarily elongated young woman that I saw at the Urban house in Yonkers. Her head rose into the top of the frame, and her legs disappeared into the bottom of it. It was called "Girl in a Plaid Garment" and was so beautiful that I was enraptured. Later it hung for many years in Urban's office on Fifty-seventh Street in New York. There was a little curl at the back of her neck and her hands were those of a Gothic saint.

The next Schieles I saw had such impact that I can see them as clearly today as I saw them sixty years ago. I remember that Mother and Father stopped to see me in Vienna for a few days during my first year at the Gerickes' and took up where they had left off in 1914. I was taken to see several new doctors; Father shipped home some cases of Tokay, and we went to see my first Schiele paintings. As on previous such occasions, I did not know how my parents met Doktor Hans Tietze and his wife, or why they showed us their Schieles. He was an art historian and, as I recall, a curator and an authority. He was a small, serious man, and his wife was dark and unsmiling. Their apartment had high ceilings and white walls. Doktor Tietze's desk stood against the wall opposite the door, and on its left hung a large painting of a black street surrounding a cluster of light buildings, an island of houses seen from above. On another wall hung the portrait of a man, sitting deep down in a large armchair, also seen as though one were standing over him.

In another room there was the picture of a dark-haired life-sized nude, lying on the floor on a sheet that spread all around her. The paintings were unforgettable, but hung low, resting on the baseboards of those high white-walled rooms below eye level, as Hoffmann once hung the Hodlers at the Secession's exhibition; they were remarkable. After that, I saw what Mary Urban called "My Madonna," which they had acquired in Vienna, and in the sixties, when I visited Dorothy Scott in Hastings-on-Hudson, I found the sinewy dark girl in the plaid garment again.

Urban had died, and so had his associate, the architect Irvin L. Scott, and I was moved to think that Urban had left his priceless Schiele Girl to them. Mrs. Scott laughed; she had acquired it only because it was a copy that Irvin Scott had made for Urban when he could not buy the original. There was no one in the world, and there probably will never be anyone, who can draw as Schiele drew, except a gifted man with a black crayon, two yards of packing paper and a photostat to go by.

The original is, as far as I know, in the Minneapolis Institute of Art—the work of a nineteen-year-old artist who was adjudged *ungenügend*, unsatisfactory and below standard.

CHAPTER 12

Doing
Three Schools a Day
in Vienna

When I accomplished my wish to study in Vienna, I should have known that Father would want to gild the lily. He could not bear to have a daughter in Vienna without having her benefit from everything that Vienna had to offer. Not only was there all that music to be heard and those dramas to be seen, but there was also *Kultur* on all sides, and his letters were full of suggestions for art history courses, poetry readings and museum lectures. What he harped on constantly was his conviction that the Hoffmann era was only a passing fad and that unless I learned to draw realistically, to relate what I saw with what I drew, I would never get anywhere. Although he admitted that even Hoffmann's pupils drew what they had seen at one time or another, he wanted me to sit before an object and draw it then and there: the more like a camera I behaved the better.

I was still going to Ferdinand Schmutzer's studio in the Akademie der Bildenden Künste on the Schillerplatz, which Father's distant cousin had arranged when Mother and I first came to Vienna, and which I had planned to give up when the Hoffmann School opened in autumn. However, Father and the cousin insisted that I combine Hoffmann and Schmutzer. The cousin, who carried weight, was a highly regarded *Sektionschef*, which I did not like to mention as I took it to mean that he did for Austria what Dr. Kinsey later did for sex in America. Professor Schmutzer was the prestigious Viennese *Radierer*, etcher, whose large portrait etchings of his friends—Pablo Casals clutching his cello, and Richard Strauss looking thoughtful—graced the walls of every better Viennese music room, while his portrait etching of Arthur Schnitzler, in neatly trimmed beard and dashing black Fedora hat, with a romantic twinkle in his eye, hung in libraries where his books lined the shelves. Schmutzer was successful, sought-after, had a lovely Vienna apartment and was socially prominent. His etching of Maria Carmi (later the perfume Princess Matchabelli) as the Madonna in Reinhart's "Miracle" hung in master bedrooms.

Schmutzer's stately Kunst Akademie was at the opposite pole from Hoffmann's Kunstgewerbeschule, and everyone who entered it learned to draw—first from plaster casts, then from models, draped and undraped—and the whole operation was exactly according to Father's picture of an artist's training. Since I could not enroll in the Academy (the one that also rejected Adolf Hitler's application) without taking a four-year course and being five years older, Schmutzer had taken me on with one other pupil to work in his studio in the Academy and not in his class. The other pupil, Rudolf Kucera, was to teach me between rare visits from Schmutzer.

Kucera gave me one look and recognized me as the chance of his lifetime to get to America and find a *Zukunft*, a future.

There I was, pleasing Father, spending absolutely traditional afternoons at the Academy drawing from empty-eyed and dusty casts of Jupiter or Minerva, from a sandaled foot, a fisted plaster hand or a Grecian capital. And while I did so, Herr Kucera, who had a single connective black eyebrow that frowned across both his eyes, concentrated on very close-up drawings of me. He was apparently not in a position to meet many Americans and decided that I was his only road to a carefree life in America, which he was paving with flattering drawings of me. It was agony, a different agony from what I later found in the Hoffmann School, but being stared at and measured with an extended charcoal stick and a squint was worse than being ignored. When drawing from casts gave way to bearded models in elderly apostolic draperies, Ferdinand Schmutzer's small studio at the Academy became an atonal nightmare of the model's wheezings, Kucera's hissed commands that I hold still and my loud self-conscious swallowings. In comparison, the vacuum-cleaner-like breathing of Professor Hoffmann was music.

After opening day at Hoffmann's *Schule*, I went there in the mornings and to Schmutzer's studio at the Academy in the afternoons, going back to the Hoffmann School every now and then in the afternoons, so that my absences were not too marked. It was at this point that Father, having thought about all my idle evening hours, insisted that a third

166

Rudolf Kucera,
my fellow pupil
at Professor
Schmutzer's
Kunst Akademie

teacher be found. I finally gave in and signed up for Professor Friedrich's women's evening life classes, which Katharine Gericke had attended. I felt very shy about the prospect of drawing people with nothing on, but I thought a crowded all-women's life class with a female model was preferable to the day, which had not yet come, when I would be alone in a small room at the Academy with the intense Herr Kucera and a male *Akt*.

I think that Father saw me learning how to draw by holding out a piece of charcoal and squinting as I measured distances between waist and knee or elbow and wrist, all this preferably on the *Apollo Belvedere*. I don't think that he visualized me in Friedrich's crowded classroom with a cadaverous old man in a loincloth holding three-minute poses because it was too cold to stand still. After a time, the old man jiggled up and down in the aisle for what were called action poses. He had a long gray beard and looked remarkably like several of the beggars that lined Vienna's streets. His body was white, when it wasn't blue from the cold; and his weather-beaten extremities, his scrawny neck and what showed of his face were a reddish-brown. Since we were unable to move about, we too were frozen, and I longed for a place in the sun where I could learn to draw and be warm at the same time.

Contrary to Father's convictions, it turned out that we only learned from Hoffmann and not from any of his pupils. Professor Friedrich, on the other hand, seemed to believe in Father's theory, since he gave us every opportunity to learn more from the other students than from him. We gathered in a *Saal*, a hall, under bright lights while the class monitor placed the model on the podium. She called the poses and turned out the light when the class was over. It was impersonal, but differently impersonal from Hoffmann. Friedrich came in, moved around among the students, remarked on the drawings he saw on our boards as he went by. The class was so crowded with students of all ages that it was more like a practice gymnasium than an art class. Everyone came in to do their own thing, while Friedrich only pointed out weaknesses in the drawings. I don't think he knew most of us apart and he certainly did not break his head about what was needed to bring out the best in us. We had enrolled in a life class and there before us was a live model. Around us were women drawing that model, all of whom seemed to benefit. There never were any female models while I was there.

After that, my life in Vienna became a conflicting three-way art study combined with an enormous amount of cross-city trotting, a forerunner of jogging, to get from one lesson to the other. The day started early, long before the winter sun was up, with Monika and my breakfast tray. In the mornings she made her bedroom entries with her behind first in a single motion that ended in an abbreviated *Knicks*, a curtsy. The tray contained a small pot of tea and two *Kipfl*, the crescent rolls that dated back to 1683 when, legend has it, a baker's boy warned Vienna that the Turks were at their gates by baking the round morning rolls in the shape of the Turkish crescent moon. The jam was Meinl's Reine Claude, greengage, and whenever I want to re-create Vienna for myself, the smell of burning coke and roasting coffee, of morning mist and lavender, all I have to do is eat greengage jam.

The new day has always seemed too exciting to me to be wasted on eating breakfast, and in any case the Viennese have a second or fork breakfast, *Das Gabelfrühstück*, corresponding to the English "elevenses," for which I gladly waited, especially since I had mine with a chocolate bar. But the disposal of breakfast in Vienna was not as easy as in New York. The john was too far away, and our washstands consisted of pitchers and bowls behind low screens with unflushable slop pails. I poured the tea down the potted plants, nibbled enough of one crescent to create crumbs and carried the remaining crescent, heavily jammed, to the birds in the *Stadtpark* on my way to Hoffmann's School. There was often *Glatteis,* glare ice, in winter, and I had to cling to the deep rustications of the buildings as I came down the Beatrixgasse's steep curve to the *Heumarkt,* or hay market. In those days it was full of horse-drawn wagons with panting, puffing horses and jingling harnesses coming through the mist. I passed Father Kneipp's fountain, which was left uncovered since he was a cold-water advocate, and the statues of various celebrities encased in wooden boxes. I flapped across the Landstrasse in my replaced arctics, past the museum and into the school, exchanged my monosyllabic *S'Gott* with my two cubicle mates and sat down before my blank sheet of paper.

I worked hard at thinking up things to put on it and gradually accumulated a few *Vogue*ish-looking fashion sketches and illustrations. I rushed home at noon for boiled beef and its revolving repertoire of sauces, and left lunch early to go to the Academy before the mocha ceremony began. The most exciting part of the day for me was the walk from the slight elevation of the Gerickes' apartment into the Karlsplatz, which had once been the battle center of Vienna's artistic conflicts. The first glimpse of the arena was the overpowering silhouette on my left of Fischer von

Erlach's triumphant Baroque Karlskirche, frowning down on the architectural trivialities below. On my right stood the *Künstlerhaus*, designed by Weber in (naturally) Italian Renaissance *Stil*, containing a double regal staircase that could receive the entire Habsburg *Hof*, the Court, on its traditional visit to the Association's annual exhibition.

Diagonally opposite stood Otto Wagner's two tiny little turn-of-the-century wedding cake city railroad stations, then being used to store tools, and Hoffmann lived in an apartment in the maze of streets behind them. Down at the end stood Olbrich's Secession, still disputed although the movement, the building and the *Stil* were more than twenty years old, and the battlefield was green again. At the right of the Secession, on the *Linke Wien Zeile*, were Otto Wagner's two mosaic apartment buildings with tiled facades and ceramic flowers climbing up to their cornices, and on the Secession's left was Adolf Loos's Café Museum where that bitter enemy of the unfunctional had installed the Charles Dana Gibson Room full of unutilitarian pompadours. It was perfectly situated for Secession watching and for the firing of darts and poisoned arrows at Hoffmann. Behind the Loos Café was the Café Heinrichshof, where hundreds of cups of coffee had gone into the founding and the founders of the Secession. All its landmarks circled a small area that I crossed each day to the Academy, where I tried to learn to draw while being drawn by Mr. Kucera. After that, I walked back to Friedrich's classes and finally back to the Gerickes'.

My life was further complicated by the Airedale puppy I bought myself. His full name, suggested by Jo Mielziner, was "Giddy Giddy Gum Gums an Artist's Life Is Not a Happy One." I called him Giddy, as I found an artist's life, with the exception of a little fear of Hoffmann, a happy one. When I asked the Gerickes whether I could keep him, they refused, with hints that his entry could only be achieved over their dead bodies, so he went to live in the *Portier*'s lodge, where he became the Jöppsells' ideal PG. Somewhere between my three schools, he took me for his daily run, which brought me up to about six cobbled miles a day. I learned why dogs in Vienna were called *Anschliessungsgründe*, grounds for connection, since Giddy and I spent much time in avoiding the men who offered to lead him for me.

Being frightened of Hoffmann in the mornings, being terrified of Mr. Kucera's frownings and close inspections of my face in the afternoons and then having to draw one of Professor Friedrich's old men hopping down the aisle was bad enough, but being trained by three different methods and three very different schools of thought was torture. Combined with the miles I covered each day and the strain of keeping my three professors secret from each other, I decided on dropping out of Friedrich's class at the end of the first semester. Being told that the left leg on one particular drawing was too long was not for me; within a short time I had become a convinced Hoffmann pupil and wanted to learn without stopping to erase and shorten a leg. I was far enough from New York to have the courage to cross Father, especially since mail that sailed on a ship across the ocean took weeks, and he might very well be on a spree of new instructions by the time word of my independence reached him.

I had not realized how quickly Hoffmann's methods would spoil me for all other teachers, especially since things at the Hoffmann School suddenly took a turn for what I thought would be the better. It was the only time I can remember that Hoffmann's fashion pupils and I pulled together and functioned as one. Their suggestion was that although we neither believed in or needed to work from a *live* model, it could do us no harm to have a look at the human body before we dressed it. Accordingly, they arranged for a model whose fee we split and got a grudging nod from Hoffmann and the use of an empty classroom down the corridor. I joined happily, knowing that this arrangement would soften my departure from Friedrich's class in Father's eye. The empty room was unheated, and the small stove we filled with filched briquettes and paper did little to keep the model from turning blue. I asked to carry the heating costs for subsequent sessions and all went well until our life group was suddenly stopped and I was given a *Rüge* from Professor Roller, the stern head. He claimed that he looked upon my financial donation toward the school heating as an act of bribery, American bribery.

A *Rüge war erteilt*, a reprimand in formal writing, was

issued, which, for all I knew, might mean expulsion. It was sent to Father, and I shuddered as I waited for his reaction. My unpredictable father thought the whole thing uproariously funny, felt full sympathy for the blue model and praise for me, who had only been trying to learn to draw as he had instructed. I was not expelled, and we continued to draw our strange elongated fashion figures without help from a live model.

I have since heard that the formidable Professor Roller issued a second *Rüge* to the beautiful Carmela Prati, which resulted in her departure from school. In her case it was not an accusation of bribery, but her throwing of what my brother Edward called a water bomb. She apparently dropped it out of one of the Kunstgewerbeschule's upper windows, from where it had gathered considerable momentum by the time it hit its target, a pompous old man who was promenading in his finery with a walking stick. Knowing that it was hard to calculate this deadly weapon's accuracy, I could only admire her. Her father, an eminent court judge, thought the incident equally funny and aligned himself with the bomb.

When Mr. Kucera said, "Tomorrow we start on an *Akt*," the long-promised nude, I sent a polite note and left him to his *Akt*. He later joined the teaching Order of the Piarists (founded by Calasanza in Rome) and sent Mother his etchings with a picture of himself weeping in the snow in a cemetery. Still later, he came out of the Order and Mother returned his etchings.

■ ■

I went back to Hoffmann's school in the afternoons, where all was calm and no one drew us while we worked. I pushed my Academy and Friedrich School sketches into a portfolio and never did learn to draw.

CHAPTER 13

Dressing Up
in Vienna

In Vienna in the 1920s Americans were "glamour pusses" of sorts, or we tried to be. We modeled ourselves after sultry actresses like Nita Naldi and Lil Dagover, or after some devastating creature whose charms were enhanced by looking as though she stood at death's door. We slouched and whispered and affected what the Viennese called *eine interessante Blässe*, an interesting pallor, the one-foot-in-the-grave look. This was done by rubbing our healthy young faces with white powder tissues, which came bound into little books and gave us a lavenderish to bluish tint. I can remember sitting in my room at the Gerickes' one long evening, holding one lighted cigarette after the other the wrong way around in my hand, allowing the smoke to rise through my fingers until thumb and forefinger were darkly tobacco-stained, all in the hope that I would be taken for a consumptive chain-smoker.

Clothes were always our problem; none of us had as many as we thought we needed, and the urge for a change had to be gratified with a new hairdo, with an inventive stocking turban wrapped around the head, with one of Katharine

Gericke's fabric flowers pinned to a shoulder, mascara on the eyelashes, a long Lalique cigarette holder or a homemade handbag gathered into a tassel at the bottom and into a drawstring at the top. No one ever wore *Confection*, a word that covered all ready-to-wear clothes, which were apparently worn only by the lower working classes and were styled accordingly. *Das Peuple*, Mrs. Gericke's word for the people who were neither cultured and talented musicians nor among those who could afford to buy tickets to listen to them, presumably sewed their own. We were all at school to learn to design clothes, not to make them, which would have taken a trade school and a long apprenticeship. The *Schule* did not even have a sewing machine or a long mirror, so our practical experience consisted in running up a few little numbers for ourselves at home, usually out of a few little old numbers. My classmates came to school in clothes that looked as though they had been handed down several times, and I wore what remained of my stolen flapper/sportswoman wardrobe, richer in riding habits than in warm school clothing. I did buy myself a blue-silk "jumper" at Stone and Blythe, when the Tutankhamen rage hit Vienna, and Hoffmann called the attention of the whole class to the *Betonung der Horizontale*, the emphasis on the horizontal, which they obediently stared at. Hoffmann, on the other hand, always wore what he conceived to be the last word in what the well-dressed (in black and white) Viennese was wearing. It was probably always the same because it was in fact the same suit, meticulously brushed and cared for, and presumably left over from his prewar visit to Charles Rennie Mackintosh in England.

In earlier pictures, before the coming of the spat, Hoffmann wore high black laced shoes, the sort that were laced through six pairs of eyelets and then changed to another six pairs of little black hooks, which speeded up dressing by a good ten minutes. He wore black wrinkled socks, a stiff collar, a light bow tie and a wilted *boutonnière* of sorts. He carried black cotton gloves and a black furled umbrella. All this turn-of-the-century finery was worn with a stiff "brush" haircut and a luxuriantly curled black moustache, setting the trend toward the total black-and-whiteness that was beginning to engulf him.

During the last years before I left New York, Mother and all my friends' mothers were cultivating the Irene Castle look, although none of them had the courage to go in for her Castle bob. Mother and Father and six enterprising friends took a series of private ballroom dancing lessons from the Castles, at which they not only learned to turkey-trot and to "hesitate," but the ladies learned to do so with one foot gracefully extended out in back with toe pointed. They all wore satin slippers with French heels that were tied with satin ribbons that crossed over the instep and wound up their legs. These were dyed to match their just-above-the-ankle-length dancing gowns and were called tango slippers.

I only heard Mother's end of the morning-after telephone rehashings, but apparently the Castles taught dancing in a hotel ballroom and the pupils went on to lively after-class champagne suppers in the hotel's dining rooms. I overheard that Vernon Castle was *wunderbar*, Father was only fair, Dr. Steel was good and so was Roswell Easton, with the disadvantage that he snapped garters, a form of coquetry that seems to have gone out with the garter. The Austrian Josef was too shy and too short to tango properly, which required stoopings and swoopings. I thought the whole thing extremely progressive and listened avidly to the descriptions of Irene Castle's Lucille gowns that were based largely on what was seen through what, as, for example, rosebuds through lace, bowknots through chiffon and embroidery through net.

In New York we took great interest in each other's clothes. We tried them on, borrowed them and copied them. But what we wore under our clothes was of even greater interest to the Viennese than our outer clothes. Our *Unterwäsche*, our underwashing, underwear or lingerie, was even then beginning to dwindle away while Vienna still clung to its prewar cotton foundations, all in unrelenting white. They had been accented here and there by pale blue or pink ribbons drawn through eyelet embroidery and tied in a tiny bow, but such seductions were the first to go, so that by the time I came to Vienna, the underwashing was bare. There was, however, always something rigid and structural in the way of a foundation or corset cover under it, which they could pin something else to. Whether it was a watch, face in, an arrangement with a fine retractable extension cord for eyeglasses or a flower, it could be anchored safely without dislodging the entire garment. On the rare occasions when I was given a corsage, I pinned it to my shoulder and suffered agonies while I held the front of my dress to keep it from being dragged down to the waist by the corsage, or off the shoulder or just off. We wore girdles instead of corsets, pink rubber circles that we stepped into and dragged up, with suitable sounds, over our hips. They were too low to pin corsages to, but we did fasten our stockings to them and yanked the girdles down at intervals during the day when they "rode up." We did this in the living room, on the street or in the front of a box at the opera, much to the dismay of our elders and the Viennese, who still wore corsets. Because these were laced as tight as a skin and attached to their stockings with garters, they could not ride up or down.

America had not yet introduced black-lace or printed or leopard-spotted lingerie, but our chemises were pink *crêpe de Chine* with narrow shoulder straps we fished for down the necks of our dresses when we were not pulling down our girdles. To these deplorable indications of what we wore under our dresses we added the powdering of our noses in public places, the combing of our hair and frequent peering into our pocket mirrors. Mrs. Gericke put up with all of it because of her reinstated *Jours* and the restored telephone, but she sniffed her disapproval.

180

Our pink chemises reached from our flat chests to the middle of our thighs and were fastened between our legs by a two-by-four-inch flap, which one of my Viennese classmates, who was having the American underwear geography explained to her, said served no purpose whatever. In any case, they were usually left open to flap by flappers, since it took three tiny mother-of-pearl buttons and the blind search for three elusive handmade buttonholes to secure them.

The only other clothes situation I knew in Vienna was that of the Gericke ladies, mother and daughter, which was unique. Large boxes arrived periodically from the Ladies Committee of the Boston Symphony Orchestra, which Professor Gericke had founded and his wife and daughter had attended religiously. The contents of the boxes always looked as though the Austrian customs officials had rummaged through them and had taken first choice. It did not really matter, since the members of the Ladies Committee were burdened by an association of ideas and sent only Boston Symphony–type evening gowns of heavily beaded or spangled black, or deep maroon satin with a swallowtail train, or bottle-green velvet with an enormously impressive *décolletage*. Nothing was ever warm or practical, and there was never the slightest possibility of hiding the long-sleeved and long-legged underwear that reposed under the Viennese white cotton bloomers, camisoles and petticoats in winter.

The Gericke ladies held the dresses up to their shoulders in front of the tilting cheval mirrors that stood in every better Viennese bedroom and murmured, "Dear Mrs. Damrosch, *liebe liebe* Miss Greene, *unsere einzige Frau Gaugen-giggel"*; then they divided the clothes into groups of two, or even three, which might conceivably be merged into one dress. As the ladies of Vienna, who had been forced to live on potatoes and starches during the war years, grew older and wider, they often combined two dresses that had fit their younger dimensions, and outlandish combinations in contrasting colors and fabrics resulted. I remember being bewitched by a Gericke guest who had inserted the back of a glossy blue-satin gown, with its slinky train, into a coral-colored dress of the type then known as a semievening gown, and the outcome combined three highly desirable features: back interest, color vibration, and a *joli mouvement*. The ladies who were not fortunate enough to be on the Gericke–Boston Symphony care list all looked as though they had been frozen in 1914 and thawed out in 1920.

A box that Mother sent for my first Christmas away from home was filled with crumpled wrapping papers, a bit of a sandwich and a list of what the box had contained: two sweaters, a woolen dress, fudge, a pair of Carceone and Manfred shoes, Robert Day Dean caramels and a single Baummarten skin. All of it had tempted the customs officials beyond endurance, and all of it was gone. I wrote and thanked her for everything and apparently took the whole loss, including the Baummarten skin, with such good grace that Mother wrote and promised a reward: we would not only shop for clothes when she came to Vienna in the summer, we would shop at the Wiener Werkstätte's Mode Salon. I walked around to the Kärntnerstrasse for more personal anticipatorial looks at the windows and set my heart on a gold-tooled black leather handbag designed by my Professor Hoffmann in such a way that the gold lines converged and created an ever-changing pattern. I inherited it from Mother some forty-two years later, when it promptly fell apart.

Mother arrived in Vienna late in June, and we went straight to the Wiener Werkstätte's Mode Salon in the Esterhazy Palais, which Hoffmann had decorated and I had never had the courage to enter. When I finally walked through the deeply recessed door between the two showcases I had mooned over so often, I found a world that was enchanting and astonishing, decorative, enormously appealing and, of course, mostly black and white. I had wanted to study with Hoffmann; I was even then in his school, but I had never realized what he was doing or what it was really all about. I felt like the stagehand who sees the opera from the auditorium for the first time, and can't believe it.

The Mode Salon was all polished white enamel with dark floor coverings or magnificent hardwood floors. Every space had been fascinatingly utilized; everything had its place and purpose long before the word "functional" had come into use. It was classically simple, with carefully designed details that only served to point up the perfection of all its proportions. Narrow black molding, small ornamentations created an intimacy that was reminiscent of Vienna's Biedermeier, and probably of Hoffmann's home in Moravia. It was all young and warm and enchanting, the diametrical opposite of that stern, unbending pepper-and-salt man, our Professor Hoffmann, who whirlwinded through class and grunted down the backs of our necks.

To look at him, one would have expected a cold and practical army-barracks type of interior, part operating room and part drafting room. Instead, the Wiener Werkstätte's Mode Salon looked as though an indulgent father had furnished it for a ravishing and dearly beloved daughter. What I had not realized was that his work contained a rich ingredient of love, love for his work, for the mediums he used, for his fellow men and for those who would move or live in the meticulously decorated spaces he was creating. It is no wonder he had no time for all our unneeded colors, unnecessary lines and unsure strokes, and no wonder he was trying to blast us away from all the unessentials and into the unmolested beauty of black and white. Seeing his work alive and in use in Vienna changed the whole situation.

Mother and I came away that first day without any of the new clothes we had longed for. We were urged to wait for the autumn *Modeschau*, fashion show, and having been shown some of Professor Wimmer's delicate sketches for the fall and winter collections, we agreed to wait. Instead of clothes, I left that day loaded down with (in a no-paper era) superbly wrapped and packaged, stringed and labeled parcels containing a whole new look for Frau Gericke's back paying-guest bedroom and my future.

The next time Hoffmann came into class, I expected a change; after all, I was living in the beginnings of a Josef Hoffmann interior and was consequently looking at him through new eyes. But he was just as stern and wordless as ever, which made me crawl back into my shell. He may have decorated homes and shops as though he were an adoring father, but he taught his classes like an irritated and disgruntled step-father. Whenever Hoffmann was particularly unyielding, I would walk around to the Wiener Werkstätte after school and look deep into his windows for solace.

When the school year ended, and we had gone through the agonizing process of having our work weighed by Professor Roller and had finally been promoted to another silent year, Mother and I went to the Waldhotel in Garmisch-Parten-kirchen in Bavaria. There Mother produced, in her strange people-acquiring way, the Bayard Hales and, a never-explained mystery, Herr Eduard Josef Wimmer-Wisgrill, who had recently been made head of the Wiener Werk-stätte's Mode Salon and professor of fashion and textile design at the Kunstgewerbeschule, where he had been a Hoffmann pupil. With him was his wife, Carla Wimmer, *née* Clara Solm, a transposition of letters that every Clara should undertake, who was the fashion *Direktrice* of the Wiener Werkstätte's Mode Salon, an enviable and weighty position. Somewhere in the background, from where he could be neither seen nor heard, was a small son called Gino, who is now a well-known Viennese journalist in his sixties.

He, like his father, is losing his hair but gradually from age, rather than from his barber's razor.

Professor Wimmer, one of the youngest staff members of the school and of the Wiener Werkstätte, was a tall, clean-shaven—I speak of his Yul Brynner-ish head as well as his face—man. I think he was blond, but such details were hard to determine in those closely-shaven-head days. He had started as a Hoffmann pupil in architecture, but what one started with in Hoffmann's school and what one came out as were two totally different things. By the time we met Professor Wimmer, he had been teaching the designing of fabrics, clothes, accessories and, if Hoffmann had his way, everything else for some years. But his forte was fashion and dressing his own wife, who modeled some of his clothes. He also designed her jewelry and an enormous hat, with all interest centered on the underside of the brim with a nest of ostriches on top.

Carla wore an exclusive Wimmer-designed Buster Brown haircut, a sensation in Austria and an upheaval in Bavaria— a straight bang across her forehead, the rest cut straight around the sides and back and just under the earlobes so that arresting ear ornaments, designed by her husband, could be worn. Such a haircut, along with the earrings and sandals, was considered proof of a liberated mind. Since she also

Professor Wimmer, wearing a hat ▪
that hides his Yul Brynner-ish head

186

wore loose batik frocks, a beaded necklace, open sandals *and* Buster Brown hair, I took her to be overliberated. She also wore an inch-wide hammered wedding band of palest yellow gold, lightly embossed with what was undoubtedly a Wimmer-in-love design. It prevented her from bending the third finger of her right hand, which made me think of her, years later, while I spent a long forenoon at Buccellati on Fifty-fifth Street and Fifth Avenue in New York, where I too had been carried away into trying on an inch-wide ring that would not come off again. The more the Italian sales gentleman fussed over me, the more congested my finger became, and since I could not very well leave with it on and since I did not want it, I had to stay. I sat with my hand held over my head, amazing the other customers, until someone remembered that Buccellati's back door opened into the Hotel St. Regis, where I ate my lunch with my finger in a bowl of ice cubes, until the ring came off. (I could, of course, have left at any time, ring and all, through the hotel's lobby and front entrance.) When the Wimmer marriage broke up, I wondered about her ring. It was presumably cut off.

Professor Wimmer had a quality, both physical and intellectual, of breathlessness. It was always as though he had just stopped running, which translated into his vivid personality and the astonishing clothes he created. His own clothes were casual and totally becoming, including a nonchalant panama hat that was rolled up when not worn so that the brim waved in a very sugar-planter-ish way when it was on. Since he wore very heavy glasses and was, I thought, in need of guidance, he bespoke my picture of Hoffmann rather more than Hoffmann did. In school, I learned later, he taught in a smock, but instead of being a black or a white smock, his was crimson, and instead of being along orphan-asylum lines, it was dramatically Italian Renaissance.

Wimmer's drawings set a style in themselves; they were always of tall graceful creatures with tiny heads, almost featureless little faces and bodies that were modishly flat under intricately layered clothes that tapered down or were gathered down into tiny feet. The small extremities created the drawstring-bag look rather than any bulkiness; hats were huge cartwheels or tight little helmets; and feet, whether they were large or small, had to be made to look long and narrow, even if it killed us. Wimmer, the pioneer, outdid himself in 1913 when he designed a three-tone sports-spectator suit; the skirt was far too long and narrow for sporting participation, but he drew his model wearing flat-heeled *boots*. Madam Lucille always wore boots that matched her clothes, which I assumed was a leg-hiding ruse, but Wimmer's street boots were cataclysmic; up to then, only a lady mounted sidesaddle on a horse could wear a boot. Not to take away from these ravishing feet, there was a large pancake of a hat.

Wimmer relied heavily on one thing going over another, and then the underthing would reappear in unexpected places. Seeing through was Wimmer's second forte; I remember

189

Some of Wimmer's dress designs, those intricately layered confections that were the last word in imaginative design, inventive fabric combinations, strange colors, and arresting silhouettes

that some years later I insisted on a room with a balcony for a stay on the Semmering so that my new Wiener Werkstätte negligee could be seen by all. It started with a long, high-waisted and short-sleeved printed silk dress in a small black, brown and white geometric, over which there was a black transparent georgette crêpe robe without fastenings that went on over the head and came to about the knees. The only trimmings were two glossy black fox cuffs, each about as wide and almost as long as a fox. I remember that it was quite impossible for me to pour my breakfast tea on the balcony. It was not, perhaps, the perfect outfit for a young girl in midsummer, but it was new, it was becoming and, although it sounds more like Mata Hari, it was entirely Wimmer.

The clothes at the Wiener Werkstätte's autumn *Modeschau* were bewitching, although the mannequins were only a shade less frumpy than the audience. They hobbled self-consciously down the long aisle in Wimmer's creations, which rarely allowed for freedom of motion. He was all for the reformed waist and free hips; women who wore his clothes could sneeze, breathe deeply and sigh. They could even start to expect a baby, but their feet were limited to a mincing, one-foot-before-the-other gait. One of the models stood out from all the rest; her expression was animated, she was blonde and she smiled. She seemed to be enjoying herself; she walked freely, was very good-looking and thin—Austrian thin, not American thin—with proper proportions. She changed her accessories with her dresses, and she wore

A sketch of me by •
Lily Steiner while I
was in Vienna

the most attractive models. I compared notes with Carmela
Prati, who sat next to us, and we both noticed that she sailed
down the long room to a point beyond us where she did a
sort of slow-motion revolution that focused the attention of
the entire room on a single guest. We leaned forward to see
who it was and realized that all the little extra smiles and
flutterings, the gyrations and pirouettes, were meant for
our Herr Professor, who sat glowing his appreciation and
pleasure.

We, his pupils, were hilarious at seeing a new Hoffmann,
blushing and flustered, but we knew in our young wisdom

and experience that it was all in vain. Our Professor Hoffmann was invulnerable, so all her wiles would get her nowhere. Due to Hoffmann's secretive ways, it was not until much later that I discovered that her name had been Carla Schmatz, and she had become the second Mrs. Hoffmann. I have since found pictures of her in Hoffmann-designed clothes, with even more layers than Wimmer allowed himself. It was the triple-cocoon look with which she carried a single artificial rose.

Mother and I ordered our beautiful Wimmer clothes unhampered by Father's taste, although some of them could be worn only when he was away. Mother selected a winter coat with oodles of fur around the cuffs, pockets and hem, but only a cold little strip of cloth around the neck. I had a suit that was fur-trimmed only after I turned the cloth collar up to my eyes to reveal a puff of fox in the center back of the neck. For once we felt as *fesch*, chic, as we wanted to be. Mother was even more abandoned than I, since she was at a frivolous age and I was at a sober one. But a Wimmer wardrobe without paternal influences was a beautiful thing.

CHAPTER 14

The Austrian Wife-Dressing Husbands

Parents usually seem elderly to their children, but my father, who had a bristly moustache and an arc of graying hair around a bald head (which he explained away as caused by the weight of his Austrian army helmet), seemed to me to be a very old man. It came as a shock, therefore, to discover that he had been forty-eight when I set off for school in Vienna, while Urban, who had a head of dense brown hair, was forty-nine and Hoffmann, with peppery hair that he cautiously combed across his head to make it look fuller, was fifty-one.

They were the influences in my life at that time and I often wondered what those three wildly dissimilar born Austrians had in common. Josef Hoffmann and Father were both parlor hypochondriacs and spoiled only-sons. Hoffmann had three sisters to do the spoiling and Father, who was a posthumous child, had only a doting mother, but they were both relatively big first-family fishes in their own little Austrian Crownland ponds and acted with suitable dignity. Furthermore, they both had a certain amount of vanity and dressed well, although Father never owned a spat and frowned on homespuns. Joseph Urban, on the other hand, wrapped himself in voluminous camel-hair coats with sashes and wore rakish Humphrey Bogart-ish hats.

Urban and Hoffmann both had blonde second wives; they were recognized architects and designers, Urban the extrovert and Hoffmann the introvert, and they sang *Wiener Lieder* while they drank *Heurigen Wein* at new-wine festivals. Father drank only *Trockenbeerenauslese*, the highest German wine category, and collected rare vintages. Hoffmann had a beautiful collection of children's toys and Urban collected Wiener Werkstätte objects. I could sometimes find that two of them shared an interest, but rarely all three. Urban and Father were incurable flirters—the Viennese called it "fleerting"—and they shone at dinner parties, whereas Hoffmann avoided entertainment and was the embodiment of staid noncoquetry. It was said that he had said he liked to be seen with beautiful women, which was hard to prove.

But the two things that all three of them had in common was their total nonparticipation in outdoor sports, with the exception of a little genteel tennis on Father's part, and the intense interest they shared, with many other Austrians, in dressing their wives. The whole business of wife dressing was an un-American sort of activity that came into practice in Vienna at the turn of the century and so exactly suited my father's tastes and temperament that he imported an overdosed version of it into his life in New York, where it was probably neither sympathized with nor understood. In his case, being a selector and purchaser rather than a designer, dressing Mother necessitated ocean crossings to England and the Continent, with railroad journeys to London, Paris and Vienna, with all their pleasant encounters. Steamer voyages in those days were an endless means of *Anschluss* and red-upholstered, betasseled and footstooled railroad compartments were the scenes of many romantic adventures. Even adjoining parlor car seats could be the first step to bed and board.

Every few months Father was suddenly overcome by a desire to see his mother, to try out some new cure or a wonder doctor, or to attend to business matters. But what he really wanted to do was to go and come via Paris, where he had studied and which he adored, and to throw himself into the joys of dressing his wife. It also gave him an opportunity to see his hatter, shirtmaker and bootmaker in London or possibly his bookmaker, to visit Poole & Co., where AN INTRODUCTION FROM FORMER CUSTOMERS WAS REQUIRED, and to look into Knize and Striberny in Vienna. Between supervising the fittings of Mother's wardrobe, supplementing his own and seeing to accessories, his trips were busy and happy. There never was any question of husband dressing; wives did not go along to peer into fitting-room mirrors over their husband's shoulders, or to take the tailor out to lunch. They did not paw through samples of shirtings or select his neckties. They stayed at home and dreaded their husband's returns, loaded with finery for them. It was a time of double fashion standards—husbands were on their own, and wives were in their hands.

However, the wife dressers that I met in Vienna were not about to go to the trouble and expense of going to Paris, or anywhere else, to order clothes for their wives, when each of them was satisfied that he himself could do better right at home than Callot, Lanvin, Poiret and Drecoll could do together. Wife dressing among the Viennese artists was in the first degree. The wife was right there at all times; she saw the sketches and stood for endless fittings, while her husband designed and directed, draped fabrics, selected colors and stuck pins into her. She never had a word in the whole transaction and it was left to her husband to add the final tasteful touches—the artificial rose, the cloud of tulle or the feather fan.

Although the three of them, Hoffmann, Urban and Father, along with Gustav Klimt, Eduard Wimmer and Kolo Moser, were all confirmed wife dressers, they went about it in different ways and with varying measures of success. Hoffmann sketched the dresses on figures that looked a little like Perrier bottles in printed stockings. Urban went wild with lamé and Russian sables, with tiers and tunics, and the covered-in-gold look. Wimmer was a dress designer by profession and, according to Carla Wimmer, her husband's clothes were the last word in imaginative design, inventive fabric combinations, strange colors and arresting silhouettes, but walking in them was out of the question. By carefully placing one foot before the other, in a mincing fashion she was just able to navigate the runway at the Wiener Werkstätte's fashion shows, and she was lifted bodily to her dressing room as soon as she came through the exit curtains.

Koloman Moser, a member of all of Hoffmann's walkouts and enterprises and a pillar of the Wiener Werkstätte's design studio, was a determined Reform Dress pioneer. He tried to eliminate the corset and thereby the entire sisterhood of Vienna's *corsetières*, the waistline and the whalebone. He went far to remove discomforts and restrictions, and made his contribution toward unhampered digestion in Vienna, but he did nothing to beautify the Viennese girl. I recently went out to the Empress Elisabeth's Hermes Villa in the *Leinzer Tiergarten* outside Vienna to see an exhibition of turn-of-the-century clothes. It was all lace and voluptuousities, cascades of velvets, waterfalls of embroidery and plungings lined with pink net. Tight waists tilted forward and upward in such a way that the moment of loosening the stays must have resembled the opening of floodgates.

And there, amid vitrines full of entrancing picture hats, shadowy veils, parasols, seductive feather boas and fans to *fleert* around, stood a showcase full of Kolo Moser's reformed female figures, with that shoulder-to-floor look of Rodin's *Burghers of Calais*. And that in a country where even the stoutest *Dirndl* has a brisk waistline and a pronounced *poitrine*, bust. Moser's Reform Dresses hung uncontrolled to the floor with added interest at the neckline, since there was none at the waist, all of which gave them the look of an impending maternity event, and ladies who wore them were treated with the utmost consideration.

Both the Frau Professor Hoffmanns wore Herr Professor Hoffmann–designed clothes. There is a photograph of Anna, the first, in a housegownish black-and-white creation, sitting on a black chair in an empty Hoffmann room. Carla, the second, having been a WW mannequin, was frequently photographed in rather more becoming and graceful clothes designed by her husband, but his real love lay in designing and wearing costumes. This he did for the WW's popular *Prêt-à-Porter* costume department, for the owners of Hoffmann-designed villas and Hoffmann-decorated apartments, and even for the house guests of the owners of his villas. Dino Wimmer remembers that as Hoffmann and his father grew older, they costumed themselves more comfortably in Arabian *Chamis* or *Abayeh,* but nothing kept them away from their favorite costume balls.

The wife dresser who came the nearest to combining his own magnificent decorative creativeness with the dressing of his wife, who never really was his wife but what Vienna called his *Lebensgefährtin,* which means a life's companion rather than a *Freundin,* which I fear my dictionary defines as a "girlfriend," was Gustav Klimt. What Emilie Flöge and he meant to each other could be seen there in his portrait of her hanging in the Museum der Stadt Wien. It is the narrow one of a tall young woman in a long green, blue and gold ornamental sheath against a curious decorative back-

Emilie Flöge, wearing one of the wonderful billowing smocks Klimt designed and she executed

ground, with the top of her head and her feet cut off by the ends of the canvas. One sees in it the perfect reconciliation of his fabric, his dress, the woman and the painter. It could only have been painted by Klimt, and it is the only portrait of her that he ever painted. The other is an early fill-in in his brother's mural.

It so happened that Emilie Flöge had a dressmaking establishment, always spoken of as a Mode Salon, which automatically placed it in the first category. She was able to execute the dresses that Klimt designed for her—lovely flounced skirts and loose sleeves, all made of fabrics that were dyed, printed, painted or embroidered according to his designs. They translated his sense of ornament into motion and looked as though they had been cut out of his sparkling canvases or as if her dresses had been set into them. Klimt himself wore great smocked smocks of his own design and her execution; they looked as though a giant orphan had bequeathed them to him.

Father was the only one of the wife dressers I knew who was a spectator type. He went to the Paris openings, ordered the clothes, went to see samples and fittings, kept in touch and should have been, one would have thought, up on trends and new looks, but what he brought home looked more or less the same from year to year. Father's taste in hats began and ended with the *cloche*, the bell, always from Reboux or Alphonsine. It was an unfortunate contraption that made Mother look like a large perambulatory mushroom, its cap made even larger by having to fit over her long, intricately arranged hair. Father had to stoop and look up under it if he wanted to see Mother's face or hear what she said. She had to tilt her head sideways when she wanted to cross a street, and she was a menace to traffic when she later drove her car from under one of them.

There is probably a lexicographer's word for a husband's preoccupation with his wife's clothes, beginning with *uxori* and ending with *vestis,* but as soon as I was old enough to be aware of what was going on around me, I thought of it as *wife dressing* and took it lightly until the day that *daughter dressing* was added. My usually gentle and sweet mother fought like a tiger, and I never did know what became of the widely hemstitched white wool dress with an orange lining that looked like what Paris considered proper for the *jeune fille.*

I do not know how the first Mrs. Hoffmann and the two Carlas or the waistless Mrs. Kolo Moser felt about the whole thing, but I do know that Mary Urban went straight to Henri Bendel when the honeymoon was over. And I know that Mother thought the whole system was what Edward would then have called "a pain in the neck." There were undoubtedly compensations; for one thing, all unaccompanied husbands, or those who were looking deeply into the eyes of a pretty model, were apt to spend more. But what good was the most expensive dress when it was unbecoming, and what good did Mrs. Moser get out of being able to breathe deeply when she looked shapeless and frumpish? Only Emilie Flöge looked as though she loved being dressed by Klimt, as who wouldn't?

Viennese husbands were never contradicted, at least not when anyone was listening, and most of them extended their wife dressing to other household interferences. They wanted to see the accounts, school reports and the new cook's references, but most of all they wanted to know what was for dinner. Some of them left their dinner-menu orders behind when they went to their studios or offices in the mornings; others came home via the markets with dinner additions under their arms, usually unsuitable. Still another school went straight to the kitchen to see (and sniff) what was simmering on the stove before they even took off their overcoats. Father liked to act the man who did not know where the kitchen was, and when he neglected to leave dinner instructions, he was bound to greet Mother with "But that was what I ate for lunch."

Hoffmann decorated beautiful kitchens and magnificent dining rooms, designed matchless table accessories and everything that had to do with festive dining, but he was far too preoccupied with his own health to be a *Feinschmecker*, a fine taster or epicure. He went off on cold-water cures and to health resorts, and never took a hand in menu making, other than from the dietician's angle. The Hoffmanns dined out at simple restaurants and entertained very little, but Urban loved his food and wine, loved to entertain, was a delightful host and gave lavish dinner parties that began and ended with champagne. Hoffmann and Father watched their weight, while Urban ate to his heart's content and gained weight accordingly. As I look back on the wife-dressing, menu-making Austrian husbands, I think the most remarkable thing about them was their wives.

CHAPTER 15

Josef Hoffmann
Paves the Way
Back to Joseph Urban

I stayed in Europe for three unbroken years while I was at my various Viennese schools. During the second summer, Father and Mother came over for their hard seats and reverential listening at Bayreuth and Edward drove out to the west coast with two classmates on what looked like a hastily assembled four wheels, some planks, a motor of sorts behind an ancient Stutz radiator and three half-barrels with pillows in them. It was at that time the American college boy's equivalent of Goethe's Grand Tour and lots of fun. The following summer, my third in Europe, a grown, tall Edward joined me to fulfill obligations in Karlsbad while Mother rendezvoused with Father in Bayreuth and we all converged on the Engadine for heavenly horseback riding, mild climbing and strenuous pastry eating on Hanselmann's terrace in St. Moritz.

Mother was to deliver me back to Vienna for another silent year of Hoffmann before she rejoined Father in New York, and Edward was to sail back with Father for his sophomore year at Princeton. We all went on to Paris together to see each other off in all our different directions, but two days before he was to have sailed, Edward died suddenly of what the doctor diagnosed as typhoid. He had teased me from the moment he was old enough; we had giggled together and found hiding places from Fräulein Martha and comfort from Father's strictness. I had been Minnihaha or Sis; and I had carried the worms and kept still when he fished. We had, for a time, a secret backwards language in which he was Drawde and I was Naillil. I knew that I would miss him for the rest of my life, but worse was watching our parents grieve. I went back to New York with them and in spite of firm intentions there never was time to go back to the Hoffmann School. My things at the Gerickes' and my Wiener Werkstätte treasures were packed and shipped to New York and Father decided that I might as well learn to draw as long as I was there. He entered me in two schools—in the Winold Reiss Art School in Greenwich Village in the mornings and in Bridgeman's life class at the Art Students League on Fifty-seventh Street in the afternoons.

It was the same color in green all over again without the chestnut trees and the Milka chocolate bars and with the difference that I did not walk past Baroque and Secession between schools. The greatest change was that Bridgeman settled me, as he settled all his pupils all his life, with a stick of charcoal, a rag of a chamois and a kneaded eraser. There were no changes of mediums or dimensions, or of any kind except that the model stood on alternate hips during alternate week-long poses. She was also rosy and warm. Bridgeman erased our drawings (therefore the chamois), drew his own over what was left of ours with the utmost skill and went on doing the same for the entire class every week.

Reiss, who was German and was, according to Father, going to replace Hoffmann for me, was a carefree, constant talker, and neither resembled or replaced Hoffmann in any way. He kept us busy with ornaments, stencils and anything we wanted to do, but Father's faith in what one learned from the other pupils was finally fulfilled as we all watched, although we did not learn how he did it, Miguel Covarrubias caricaturing us. Reiss never changed our medium from primary poster colors, or our dimension from that of half a Bainbridge illustration board, but we did change our location. In spring we all moved from the Greenwich Village school to the Winold Reiss Art School at Woodstock, New York, where everyone got lovely tans. Mother rented the Richard Le Gallienne house, which sounds more impressive than it was, and my studies went on between country-imposed interruptions, as, for example, the exercising of Saint Francis, my horse, or the searching for Saint Patrick, my Irish setter puppy, who required hours of being hunted for every day. Their sanctifications were a kennel-stable coincidence.

I had no way of knowing, and I never did find out, how and when the Hoffmann School would have ended for me.

It was a bridge I had never crossed and a subject we never conjectured about while we were there. None of us even knew whether there would be some sort of graduation or whether Hoffmann would simply come in one day and tell us, via Haerdtl, that we were on our own. But I did know that I would have stayed as long as I possibly could and that I would never find the same inspiration and impetus anywhere else. I was no sooner home than I longed for Vienna and the continued teaching of J. Hoffmann as I had never longed before. He may not have been a bed of roses or everybody's cup of tea, but once a Hoffmann pupil, always a Hoffmann pupil; in spite of all the buffetings and the uprootings, the silences and the disregardings, he was not to be replaced. He was not even a person one could write to or pour one's heart out to; having manipulated us out of what we were doing and what we thought we wanted to do, we could not go back to it. I lost all desire to paint Persian miniature *Stil* illustrations, to do Memling *Stil* Madonna Christmas cards or Erté *Stil* fashion plates; I left Father's two New York schools after a year, rented half a studio and tried to make myself "paint it on the wall" or "cut it in wood." Father gradually went back to his wine-buying/Mother-visiting European travel schedule, while Mother became the president of her charity.

When we had come back from Paris, I found the strange bedroom that I had once hoped was what J. Hoffmann would have done. I added the WW furnishings from the Gerickes' back bedroom and achieved something that was still not exactly what I had come to recognize as the Hoffmann *Stil*, but it was nearer. I had Dagobert Peche's "Water" on the walls, a precise gold-and-white-diamonded geometric paper with a Peche gold-leafed mirror that exactly filled three diamonds. There were WW bolsters and pillows, and very little glowing Biedermeier furniture preserved the required Hoffmann emptiness. After a time I took over Edward's room, where I had everything from cabinets, desk, bookcases and shelves built in (all in white of course) and spread my Hoffmann objects on mantel and tea table around the gas logs. When my old friends came to see me, they said I was *more different* than ever. I felt different and I felt lost.

When I was highest and driest, Pepperl Urban called up with a job for someone versatile. While I had been away, he had taken the Metropolitan Opera, Flo Ziegfeld, W. R. Hearst, the Huttons and Palm Beach by storm. In order to house all his projects, he had recently acquired a great black hulk of a shabby loft building in Yonkers, which contained an unshaven man-of-all-work, Phil Kuss (kiss), and the Hungarian painter Jambor. I had, in the meantime, learned to drive and had the use of Father's gray Pierce Arrow sedan, which, if it could be judged as a horse is judged, had promising width between the eyes and a generous brainpan. Urban

Just back from Vienna and learning to drive ■
an enormous Pierce Arrow. The dress was my design.

had contracts for the Palm Beach Bath and Tennis Club, the Montmartre Theater, the Ziegfeld Theater and Metropolitan Opera settings. He also had a little beach cottage for the Huttons on his board, and said *Jeessus* as usual.

I drove myself at dawn each morning, for two years, to paint at Urban's scenic studio in Yonkers, which moved from the dreary loft to a city-block-long renovated skating rink within a short time. The number of employees was increased, opera and Ziegfeld Follies settings were executed there, and I painted my murals for various clubs and hotels and the Plaza Persian Room on the floor with the help of various members of the staff. Being a Hoffmann pupil, I started with the Montmartre Club's curtains and leaped from gigantic to mini dimensions, from my 64,000-foot mural in the Ziegfeld Theater, to designing small-scale upholstery fabrics and place cards for Mrs. Hutton.

During all those years of working in New York, I returned to Vienna for our holidays and continue to love it as ardently as I had long ago. We always lived at the Bristol, where the young apprentices became the dignified captains, and our class monitor Oswald Haerdtl became Professor Haerdtl, with his own school in the Hochschule für Angewandte Kunst in Wien, the good old Kunstgewerbeschule. Hoffmann, who had always worried about his health, lived to a robust eighty-six. His powerful work, his accomplishments and achievements were retarded by the hardships and setbacks of two world wars and the tragedy of losing his closest associates and friends in 1918. His WW had to close in 1931,

- In the country, on my return from Vienna, with the wirehaired dachshund who was Giddy's successor

■ ■

but he went it alone, setting the pace in his dignified im-
personalized way, and Mela Haerdtl says her only regret,
as it is mine, is that his own individuality made it impossible
for any of us to approach him, to show him our admiration
and affection.